SOMETHING DISCOVERED

FUNERALS AND WEDDINGS ~ BOOK TWO

BERNADETTE MARIE

5 PRINCE PUBLISHING

Published by 5 PRINCE PUBLISHING & BOOKS, LLC

PO Box 865, Arvada, CO 80001

www.5PrinceBooks.com

ISBN digital: 978-1-63112-266-8

ISBN print: 978-1-63112-267-5

Cover Credit: Marianne Nowicki

To Stan,
Who could have imagined I would discover the keys to my future when
you walked past me on that fateful August afternoon? I love you.

ACKNOWLEDGMENTS

T, N, G, S, J: Because of each of you, I have discovered true happiness.

Mom and Sissy: It has been an adventure discovering what we are capable of. We rock!

Cate: I discover something new every time you edit me. You continue to be an amazing educator.

To my Book Hive and Betas: Thank you for always accepting the task put before you.

To my Readers: Thank you for your outpouring of love and support. I love writing for you.

THE MATCHMAKER SERIES

Matchmakers

Encore

Finding Hope

THE THREE MRS. MONROES TRILOGY

Amelia

Penelope

Vivian

THE ASPEN CREEK SERIES

First Kiss

Unexpected Admirer

On Thin Ice

Indomitable Spirit

THE DENVER BRIDE SERIES

Cart Before the Horse

Never Saw it Coming

Candy Kisses

ROMANTIC SUSPENSE

Chasing Shadows

PARANORMAL ROMANCES

The Tea Shop

The Last Goodbye

HOLIDAY FAVORITES

Corporate Christmas

Tropical Christmas

THE DEVEREAUX FAMILY SERIES

Kennedy Devereaux

Chase Devereaux

Max Devereaux

Paige Devereaux

FUNERALS AND WEDDINGS SERIES

Something Lost

Something Discovered

Something Found

Something Forbidden

Something New

SOMETHING DISCOVERED

CHAPTER 1

One of the perks of moving back to Colorado, Alex thought as he pulled his gym bag from his backseat, was being near *the team*. Who could have imagined when he'd flown out in February to attend their coach's funeral that he'd be back home for good, and that Sunday mornings would be for playing basketball with the boys again?

"Yo, Al," he heard his sister's voice from across the parking lot.

He watched as Sarah retrieved her bag and a ball and headed toward him. The additional perk was that he got to spend more time with his sister, too.

"I can't believe you still wear those sweatpants," he teased as she neared him wearing a ratty pair of University of Wyoming sweats.

"You know I never throw out treasures. Just think if I did, I'd have stopped talking to you years ago." She nudged him with her elbow.

"I can't decide if that's a compliment or a jab."

"Oh, hell, bro, I like you. Now, c'mon. I have a lot of caffeine in my veins and you and your friends need an ass-whooping."

And usually it was an ass-whooping they got if they were on a team opposite his sister. Though he and his old teammates had been hailed as some glory team in their time, none of them held a candle to Sarah.

Five years his junior, she'd grown up as his practice partner. Many late nights had been had in the driveway throwing free throws and layups. Perhaps she owed her skill to him.

They walked through the front door of the YMCA and toward the gym, where he could already hear his friends razzing one another.

Their voices carried down the hall, and it brought a smile to Alex's mouth.

He'd been gone since he'd graduated from college. Luck had given him a job in Philly, which eventually moved him to Jersey before he landed in Boston. Seeing the guys, who were brothers to him, was rare until last February when Alex had returned to Colorado for Coach's funeral. The five of them picked right back up where they'd left off.

As he turned the corner to the gym, he smiled. Craig was now married to Coach's daughter, and they were expecting a baby. Ray was a divorcée with two kids and it was his week with his kids, Alex noticed, when he saw Connor and Charlotte running through the gym bouncing a ball.

Toby tied up his fancy high tops, which Alex thought was out of character for the millionaire C.E.O. Other than his house and his car, nothing said the man was worth a lot. He was humble to the core.

Bruce, who lived in Alex's basement, in the house he'd bought from Craig when he'd decided to relocate back to Colorado, saw them walk through the door. And, as was the norm, he bee-lined for Sarah, bear hugging her and planting a noisy kiss on her cheek, before winking at Alex because he knew it drove him crazy.

Yes, this was his crew. He'd been back permanently for three months, and he'd fallen into a groove—they all had. As if the past decade since they'd graduated had never existed, they'd all melded right back into *the team*, and Alex was grateful to have them.

Toby looked up at Alex as he set his bag on the bench. "How's your mom doing?" he asked sincerely.

Alex smiled. "Great. After she recovered from her surgery, there's been no stopping her."

"That's good to hear." Toby stood up and swapped places with Bruce who sat down next to him.

"Do you bring your sister every week just to torment me?" he asked as he slipped his feet into his high tops.

"You know if you ever made a move on her she'd flatten you."

Bruce wiggled his brows. "She's in love with me. Always has been."

"In your dreams."

"She keeps me happy in my dreams." Bruce laughed and Alex shook his head. If Bruce ever laid a hand on his sister, he'd kill him. But for today, he'd take the ribbing.

Alex took his time putting on his shoes and just listening to his friends. When he'd finally looked up again, he saw Craig's wife Rachel walk through the door, and in tow was her best friend Catherine.

She caught Alex's casual glance, but whatever flashed in her eyes, it didn't give him warm fuzzies.

Catherine Anderson had always been a mystery to him. She was extremely protective of Rachel. That was understandable. Rachel had been surrounded by horny teenagers her entire life, since her father was a college basketball coach, and he had the team over often. Catherine had never much been one of Alex's fans, and he probably deserved that dishonor.

When Craig was out of the scene, after they'd graduated from college, Alex had moved in on Rachel. Though he'd been hopeful, it hadn't ended with him and Rachel in any kind of romantic partnership.

But in the last year, since Rachel's dad died and she'd fallen back in love with and married Craig, Catherine was around more, and they'd had their friendly exchanges. Hell, she'd even accepted his invite to his party over the Fourth of July.

Her eyes darted away, and he realized now he'd been staring. Well, no wonder the woman was creeped out by him. It was too bad too, he thought as he joined the others in the center of the court. Catherine had been on his mind a lot lately, and he'd like to try and mend that friction between them.

The teams were divided and Alex lined up for the tipoff.

Just as he jumped for the ball, his fingertips grazing it and sending it forward, he realized Catherine had stood from her seat to remove her coat and the ball flew right into her face.

CHAPTER 2

*E*verything flashed red and then went to black. Catherine felt the impact of the ball, blinked once, and staggered backward.

A set of arms came around her before she fell back into the bleachers, and eased her to her seat.

She could taste blood, and then she could feel it run over her lips.

"Take this," Rachel's voice said as a towel was thrust into her hand.

She held it to her face.

"Ease your head back a bit," another voice said, and she recognized it at Alex's. His voice was in her ear, and she knew it was his arms that had caught her.

As she tried to take in a breath, she realized it was hard to do because everyone surrounded her. When she fully opened her eyes, there were six sets watching her, and she could hear Ray talking to his kids on the other side of the gym, telling them to sit down, stay out of the way, and be quiet for the moment.

"I'm fine," Catherine managed through gritted teeth. "Everyone back up."

She sat up, still holding the towel to her face.

Everyone moved but Alex. "I'm so sorry. I'll go get you some ice. Do you need to go to the hospital?"

She assessed the situation for a moment. "I'm fine. This will stop shortly. But yes, I'd like some ice."

He nodded. "I'll be right back."

She didn't know if she'd need the ice or not, but at least it got him out of her way so she could decide just how bad she'd been hurt.

It wasn't the first time she'd been hit in the face with a ball. Hell, she was a softball player, a catcher. She'd taken plenty of balls to the face. This stung, and made her bleed, but it didn't mean she'd suffer over it.

Pulling the towel from her face, she realized her nose still bled. Tipping her head back slightly, she pressed the towel back to her face.

Alex rushed back into the gym with an icepack wrapped in brown paper towel. "Here."

"Hold on to it for a moment," she said, closing her eyes to keep calm.

He sat down next to her. "Shit, I owe you big now."

"No kidding."

"I'll buy you dinner," he promised.

"If I have two black eyes, I'm not going to want to go out in public." Then the thought occurred to her, two black eyes were not going to be an option. "I have a job interview tomorrow."

"Shit. Shit!" Alex bit out the words. "Cath, I'm so sorry."

She hated that shortening of her name—usually, except when Rachel said it. Why when he said it, especially in that moment, did she find it endearing?

Maybe it was because in that moment, it seemed as if Alex were more vulnerable than she was, even with a bloody towel pressed to her face.

"You all just go play your game. I'm going to be fine. I've had this happen before," she encouraged them.

Slowly they all walked back onto the court, but again, except Alex.

His dark eyes were filled with worry, and didn't the humble side of him pique her interest?

"Can I get you anything else?" he asked.

"I'm going to take you up on that dinner. I sure as hell am not going to want to cook tonight. But you'll have to bring it to my house."

"It's a date," he said and a worried little smile crossed his lips as he headed back out to the court.

Rachel scooted closer to her as Catherine pulled the towel away from her face, checked for fresh blood, then she put the ice pack on the bridge of her nose.

Rachel studied her. "Are you sure you're okay?"

"Freak accident. I'm fine."

"You're going to let him into your house?"

"He let me into his."

"Yeah, but you seriously just invited him over."

Catherine narrowed her gaze at Rachel over the ice pack. "If I have to go into a job interview tomorrow with black eyes, then I'm damn well going to get dinner out of it."

"With Alex?"

"With Alex," she said firmly, though even she felt the sting of it.

The game began again, but Catherine could see that it wasn't going to be the same hour of fun she'd witnessed in weeks past. Alex's attention was directed toward her.

WHEN THE ICE PACK WAS NO LONGER COLD, SHE REMOVED IT FROM her face. She could feel the stiffness around her nose. As soon as she got home, she'd assess the situation. When the hour the group had reserved the court for was almost up, Catherine rolled up the towel and slipped it into her bag with the ice pack.

They called the game, and Sarah, Bruce, and Ray had won for the week.

Catherine watched as Craig moved to his wife and helped Rachel to her feet. He rested his hand on her swollen belly, and kissed her sweetly. Catherine had to admit, she was still getting used to seeing them together again, even after seven months. There was a part of her that couldn't believe Rachel had gotten involved with Craig again, but Rachel had always been more resilient than Catherine had. Heartache, depression, and near death experiences were all in a day's work for Rachel. Not that she didn't take those things seriously, she sought professional help. But Catherine would always feel the need to protect her.

"Are you going to be okay?" Rachel asked Catherine one more time.

"I'm fine."

"Okay, we're headed to my mom's for lunch. Are you sure you don't want to join us?"

Catherine shook her head. "Especially now," she laughed. "Have a good day. I'll talk to you tomorrow."

Rachel hugged her, and then with Craig's arm around Rachel's waist, she waved goodbye and headed out of the gym.

Catherine picked up her bag and waved as Sarah headed toward the gym to get in her workout. It humored her. Playing basketball and working out were the last things on Catherine's mind.

"I don't know whose towel I bled all over," Catherine said to the four men still in the gym taking off their shoes.

Toby looked up at her. "I think it was mine. But I have a million towels. Don't feel like you need to bring it back."

"I'll replace it."

He shook his head. "I seriously have a million of them."

Catherine laughed. "Okay. Well, I'll see you guys later."

She walked past them and out the door, but slowed when she heard her name called.

Alex ran from the gym, his shoes in his hands and his bag unzipped, slung over his shoulder.

"One more time," he said. "Are you okay?"

"I'm fine. No sweat."

"You have no idea how bad I feel."

"It was an accident."

"Tacos?"

Catherine laughed at the statement that was so out of place.

"What?"

"I mean can I bring over tacos? For dinner," he reminded her.

"Tonight?"

"Sure. You have to let me do something to make up for what I did to you."

She gave it some thought as she chewed her bottom lip. "Okay. Six o'clock, and bring Coronas and limes."

Without another word between them, she headed out of the YMCA and to her car.

CHAPTER 3

*C*atherine stood in the bathroom and examined her face. Sure enough, she was going to have a lovely set of black eyes. She supposed she should be grateful, she didn't have a broken nose. Then again, leave it to Alex Burke to be so clumsy to hit her in the face at a friendly game of basketball.

She blew out a breath.

He'd been sincere in his angst, but she supposed it would never be enough where Alex was concerned. He was a cocky man, and he'd been a cocky teenager too. Just thinking about the way he'd moved in on Rachel after he'd graduated college made her stomach clench.

Catherine turned off the light and walked out to her kitchen. She'd set the table for tacos, though she should just take the bag she assumed Alex would bring, and send him on his way.

She pulled a glass down from the cupboard, filled it with ice and water, then sat back down. Knowing Alex was going to be knocking on her door at any moment seemed to stir her up, and she wasn't sure what that meant.

Since he and *the team* had graduated college, she'd had

nothing but a deep-seated dislike for them—especially Alex and Craig.

Craig had disappeared after his father had come back into his life, so briefly and for the first time. He'd become a genuine asshole, broke Rachel's heart, and took off. Then Alex stepped in. What he'd hoped to achieve, Catherine would never be sure, but what young man didn't want what his friend had left?

Alex never had a shot. By the time he had wormed his way into her life, Rachel had begun cutting herself, drinking, and eventually attempted suicide as a means to get over the trauma of having found her brother when he'd committed suicide.

The whole situation was messed up.

Eventually, Rachel's parents sent her away to get help. When she emerged, she went to college to become a therapist and help people like herself. Catherine couldn't be more proud of her best friend.

She'd admit that Craig had pulled his life together and she gave her blessing to him marrying Rachel. But still, she hadn't found it in her heart to forgive Alex for being some douchebag and wanting his turn.

The very thought of it that way made Catherine sick.

It wasn't supposed to be a problem. He lived in Boston.

When he returned for Rachel's father's funeral, Catherine was cordial to him, for Rachel's sake. All the while knowing he'd be headed back to the East Coast and out of their lives.

Then he moved back to Colorado and bought Craig's house when Craig moved in with Rachel.

Seriously, there was no getting rid of the man.

She'd tried to befriend him, especially when they'd all surrounded Rachel with love and support, but now that she was sporting two black eyes and a bruised nose, her thoughts went back to him being that douchebag.

Catherine jumped when the doorbell rang. She bit down so hard her jaw hurt as she rose and walked toward the door.

It was a mistake to invite Alex Burke to her house. It was like inviting the devil to cross the threshold and enter.

Catherine pulled open the door, her vision blurred by anger that had been brewing for over a decade. But when she saw him standing on her front porch, a casserole dish covered in foil, and a bag dangling from his arm, in which she could see the tops of the beers she'd suggested he bring, her shoulders dropped.

"You showed up," she said curtly.

"Damn, I did a number on you, didn't I?" He looked at her and she wondered if her attitude was showing. Oh, he'd done a number on her, and hadn't she worked herself up over it? "That's going to turn purple by morning."

It was then she realized he was talking about her nose.

She lifted her fingers to the tender skin. "I'll figure out some makeup."

"Can you take the bag? My fingers are going numb."

Catherine reached for the bag. "Did you actually make tacos?"

Alex nodded. "Not too hard. If we eat soon, the shells won't be soggy either. Can I come in?"

Catherine stepped back and let him pass. She shut the door and led him to the kitchen. "I thought we'd just eat in here. Is that okay with you?"

"Fine with me," he said as he set the dish on the table. "This is a nice place."

"I'd say we could eat on the patio, but with the new builds, if the wind picks up the dirt blows."

"Next year you'll be able to entertain."

They were making small talk about her newly built town-house and the flaws of new construction. Was that all they were going to be able to talk about?

Alex took the bag from her, which she still held.

"Do you have a cutting board? I'll cut the limes."

Catherine blinked. "Yes." She moved to the island, opened the drawer, and pulled out the cutting board. Turning around, she opened another drawer, and retrieved a knife.

Holding it out to him, she realized she had a firm grip on the handle, and he'd scanned a slightly horrified look over her before she set it down and walked back to the table.

"In the bottom of the bag are some bowls with cheese, tomatoes, onion, and sour cream. I'll cut the limes for the beers and we should be set."

Catherine pulled out individual glass bowls, removed their lids, and set them on the table as Alex cut the limes. No doubt he could feel her tension clogging the air.

"Bottle opener?" he asked and she snapped up her head.

"Drawer with the knives."

Alex retrieved the opener and two wedges of limes. At the table, he set the wedges on a plate, took out two beers, and opened them. "Hopefully this won't explode all over," he laughed as he picked up one of the wedges and slipped it into the bottle.

He handed her the bottle, then did the same with the next.

They both watched the slight foam that created. When they didn't overflow, they both let out a sigh.

"Here's to forgiveness," he said smiling down at her.

"Forgiveness?" Did he know exactly how she felt about him?

"Yeah. I hope you forgive me for today. Seriously, that was a lot of misguided fate for that tipoff to hit you. You have no idea how bad I feel."

Looking into those dark sympathetic eyes, Catherine decided she wanted to know exactly how bad he felt.

CHAPTER 4

*A*lex sipped from his beer. He certainly wasn't welcome, and he couldn't help but wonder why she'd even invited him.

The bruising from getting hit with the ball was growing darker, and it tugged at his heart, but not as much as seeing the anguish in the blue eyes that diverted his attention.

Well, they'd eat and he'd be on his way. He wasn't sure what else he could do to extend the olive branch to her.

"Should we eat?" he asked and she pulled out a chair and sat down. "I didn't make anything spicy. I wasn't sure your tastes."

"Pretty plain."

"That works for me."

Alex pulled the foil off of the dish. "How about spoons for the toppings?"

Those blue eyes lifted to meet his. "Drawer next to the knife drawer."

Alex moved through the kitchen, retrieved the spoons, and returned. Catherine had taken two tacos and set them on her plate. He figured he had at least twenty minutes for her to eat and drink the beer before she kicked him out. He'd try to make the most of it.

As he sat down, he set the spoons in each of the bowls. Taking two tacos for himself, he set them on his plate. "You said you had a job interview tomorrow. What happened with your job with the school district?"

Catherine picked up her beer and took a long pull, then pressed her hand to her chest as she swallowed. He knew then that she had swallowed down too many bubbles. A moment later she set the bottle down and let out a breath.

"I left after the active shooter situation with Rachel."

He should have known that much, and now he was sorry he asked.

God, hadn't Rachel been through enough? First she finds her younger brother after he committed suicide, she gets involved with one of her dad's basketball players and gets caught, then she turns to drinking and tries to commit suicide after having taken to cutting herself. But all that had been a decade before. She'd gone on to help people. Then she fell in love, found out she was pregnant, and then one of the people she helped nearly got her killed when he entered the school with a gun and locked himself in her office with her. And Catherine had been outside the building when it had all gone down.

No wonder she didn't want to work there anymore.

"I guess I can see why you need a change of pace," he said as he scooped sour cream from the bowl and added it to his tacos.

"Not that its safer somewhere else. I mean it can happen anywhere."

"True. But I suppose it'll always be fresh in your mind when you walk into a school."

Now when she lifted her eyes, they seemed to hold an under-standing. "Right."

"So what is the new job?" he asked as he bit down into his first taco.

She laughed as she lifted her taco toward her mouth. "Data entry for a pharmaceutical company."

"Interesting."

"Boring."

"And that's what you want?"

She took a bite of her taco, and set it back down as she chewed. Then she washed down her bite with a pull from her beer. "Yes. No." Why did she want to even justify it for him? "I just know I need a change."

"I get that," he said as he leaned back in his seat and took a long drink from his bottle. "I had a great job in Boston. A beautiful condo. A nice nest egg. And a woman to share it with. Now I'm here, living in Craig's old house, glad that Bruce rents the basement to help with the mortgage. But I'm happier than I was six months ago. The job I have isn't one I thought I'd have, but it's good. I can leave it at the office when I walk out the door."

Catherine batted her eyes. "Yes. That's what I want. I want to know that when I leave work I don't take home the worries. I need time away from politics, parents, kids, and problems. And that's why I hope Rachel never goes back."

"Do you think that's what will happen?"

She shrugged. "A bullet through your shoulder should make you never want to go back into a school. But she'll want to help more people. I just hope the baby will change her mind."

"I'm sure it will."

Catherine broke off a piece of her taco shell and popped it into her mouth. "What happened to your job, your condo, and your woman?" she asked, and Alex looked at the bottle in his hand, then set it on the table.

"Well, the woman got involved with some other men."

"Oh," she drew out the word.

"Yeah. It seems like everyone was with her, but she was living with me." The pain of it was still fresh and that stung. "I started drinking, that cost me my job. When I came out for Coach's funeral, I'd hit rock bottom. Then when my mom was going to have surgery, and Craig was going to marry Rachel, I saw a new opportunity. It was the right time to move back home, buy Craig's place, and start over. Now I'm glad I did. Once again, because of Coach, I have my brothers back. I've missed them, and what we had."

Catherine leaned in on her arms. "It's easy to be envious of what you have with them."

He shook his head. "No, I think the friendship you and Rachel have is the enviable one. You've always had her back and you still do. You're very protective of her."

She bit down on her bottom lip and worried it. "I might be a bit too protective of her."

"That's your right. You've seen her through a lot of shit."

"I have."

He lifted his beer toward her and she picked up her bottle. "Here's to those friendships that become family. And to the families that merge."

He tapped his bottle to hers and then drank down his beer, but she kept her eyes focused on him, never taking another sip.

CHAPTER 5

*C*atherine pushed open her front door, her purse falling from her shoulder, the bag of groceries falling over at her feet, and her cell phone balanced on her shoulder.

"Ya?"

The giggle on the other end told her who was waiting to talk to her.

"So how did the interview go?" Rachel asked.

Catherine gripped her phone, dropped her purse inside the door, and picked up the bag of groceries. She kicked the door shut with her foot and walked to the kitchen.

"Oh, I suppose it went okay. You know, I'm covered in make up, which I don't usually wear. I can't smile too wide, or my nose hurts. And still, the little bit of dark comes through the makeup. I'm going to say I look exhausted with dark circles under my eyes. So, they either don't want a battered and bruised woman, or one that stays up all night."

"You didn't get the job?"

Catherine hoisted the bag up onto the counter. "I don't know. They'll call me sometime this week. But I don't know if I want it anyway. What the hell did I do? I quit my job. I left my career."

18

"I'm sure they'd understand if you called and changed your mind," Rachel's voice was soft on the other side.

"You think I want to walk back into a school any time soon after what happened to you?"

She heard the sigh. "It was a freak accident."

Catherine pulled out a chair from the kitchen table and sat down. How Rachel could say something like that was beyond her. She was right. Rachel had been hit with gunfire from the police, not from the young man who had shot out windows at the school. He hadn't shot anyone, but they'd ended his life right in Rachel's office. No, it was too much for Catherine to even consider.

"I made the right choice," she said. "I just need to find my next thing."

"And you think it's in data entry?"

Catherine chuckled. "Alex and I discussed the joys of having a boring job that you leave at the office when you go home. That's what I need right now."

"I get that," Rachel said. "Okay, now, the second part of my call. How was your dinner with Alex?"

Smiling, Catherine stood and walked toward the bag of groceries she'd carried in. She set her phone on the counter, hit the speaker button, and began to put the items away.

"It was awkward," Catherine admitted.

"How so?"

"It just was. Rach, I've spent most of the time I've known the man despising him. Then he was out of sight, out of mind for a decade. But now he's back. I'll admit that for the first few months he was around, I probably let my guard down. He was comforting when you were going through your things," she explained hoping not to stir up anything deeper.

Catherine opened the refrigerator and began to load in the fresh produce. "I want to really be mad at him for my face looking like this, but I think he was horrified in his own right."

"So, it was bad?"

"No. I said it was awkward."

There was a brief silence, as if Rachel had run out of things to say. Then Catherine heard her take a breath. "He invited everyone over on Sunday for dinner. He and Ray are going to smoke some meat or something this weekend. He asked me to invite you."

Catherine shut the refrigerator door. "He couldn't ask me himself?"

"Well, funny enough, when I asked him about dinner last night, he said it was awkward."

That make Catherine laugh again. "At least it was mutual."

"Will you go?"

"I don't know. I'm just an extra wheel."

"Since there are no couples but me and Craig, there are lots of extra wheels. Please."

"I'll think about it. You never know what might happen to me and my face between now and Sunday."

Alex sat in a lawn chair in the back yard, a beer in his hand, admiring the bright orange sunset. One thing was for sure, he'd missed watching the sun go down behind the Rocky Mountains while he lived in Boston.

Since he'd bought Craig's house, he'd made it a ritual to sit out back and catch as many sunsets as he could.

The peaceful moment was marred by headlights pulling into the drive, and Bruce parking his car.

Alex watched him step out and retrieve his gym bag from the back seat.

"Mind if I join you?" he asked as he opened the side gate and walked into the yard.

"Don't mind at all. There are beers in the fridge."

"Nah. I got me a nice cold Gatorade," Bruce laughed as he pulled one of the chairs from around the patio table out next to where Alex lounged, and straddled it backward. He opened the lid from his bottle and took a swig of the blue liquid. "Never gets old, does it?" he said looking out over the horizon.

"Never. I invited everyone over for dinner Sunday."

"Cool. Sarah said she was coming."

Alex turned his head, a fixed glare in place at the mention of his sister. "You talked to my sister?"

"She was walking out of the gym as I was walking in," he said matter of factly.

Alex nodded slowly and then mindfully sipped from his beer. "Rach said Catherine would think about it."

"Dinner last night didn't go so well?"

"Awkward."

"Well you did give her two black eyes."

"It was an accident."

"I was there. I know. But damn, of all the people, huh?"

Yeah, he thought. Of all the people he could mess up around, it was always going to be Catherine Anderson. She didn't need any more reason to dislike him, though he thought there should be some kind of time limit on it. He understood Catherine's dislike of the whole team, in general. She was a protector, and when that many horny teenagers are hanging around, any sensible girl would want to shield their friend. And, Alex had made his move on Rachel after Craig left back then, but in his head, he remembered his intentions being a little more wholesome than Catherine might have thought they were.

Either way, she'd held onto that grudge for a very long time. And wasn't it a shame?

The beautiful blonde with the magnificent smile had been on Alex's mind since he'd seen her at Coach's funeral. He'd thought there was a breakthrough between them when they'd all rallied around Rachel on the Fourth of July, when the sound of fireworks triggered the trauma she'd gone through with the active shooter at the school. Catherine had let him ease in, wrap his arm around her, and they'd even settled on the couch together. Maybe that night had done them all in.

Still, awkward wasn't how he wanted to talk about his time with Catherine.

He sipped from his beer. Once upon a time, Alex Burke had game, maybe it was just time to try and get it back.

CHAPTER 6

*C*atherine pulled up in front of Alex's house and parked on the street. The driveway was filled with now familiar cars, but she couldn't make herself want to get out of the car and walk to the back yard. It was silly really. The men, to whom the cars belonged, had been in her life since she was a teenager. But everyone changed in a decade, didn't they? She didn't belong there now any more than she had when she was just fifteen hanging out at Rachel's house.

Back then she'd been the annoying best friend of the coach's daughter. Annoying because she'd wanted Rachel's attention, and often the star center, Craig, got it. Now he had her full attention as Rachel's husband. Annoying because she always tried to be the voice of reason in Rachel's ear, and sometimes that caused a rift between them.

She contemplated driving on and no one would be the wiser. Surely she was just an add-on invitation. Then she thought about Rachel. She'd told her she'd be at the damn barbecue, and there she was.

She let out a sigh. And in true form, even when *the team* was

BERNADETTE MARIE

around, Rachel made sure to include Catherine. She owed her the courtesy of showing up.

Pulling down her visor, she checked herself in the mirror. Her face had healed, and only the very slightest yellow tinge still colored her skin. She'd never know if that was what kept her from getting the job in data entry, but it was in the past. Alex hadn't meant to hit her with the ball.

Finally, she pulled the handle on the door and pushed it open. If she was uncomfortable, she could just go home, she thought as she stepped out. But she knew there was nothing to be uncomfortable about. She'd been around them all since the coach's funeral. It was just one more back yard barbecue.

Catherine closed the door and walked around the back of her car, stopping at the edge of the yard one more time to contemplate what she was doing.

"Are you coming on back?" Alex stood in the driveway and watched her.

She hadn't seen him standing there until he spoke. "Yeah. It smells good," she said.

"Stinking up the neighborhood and making them all jealous," he laughed.

He was dressed in a pair of khaki shorts and a beige shirt that buttoned down the front, casual and airy in the August heat. His sunglasses shielded his brown eyes, and his hair was longer than she'd remembered. Or maybe it had fallen over his forehead in the heat.

In one hand he held a beer and the other a glass of wine.

"Everyone is around back," he said holding out the glass of wine. "This is for you. Toby brought it, so you know it's good stuff."

She took the glass, brushing Alex's fingers with her own as she did so. "Were you waiting for me?"

"I saw you drive up," he admitted.

Catherine took a sip of the wine. "This is nice."

"It is, isn't it? He invested in some Palisade winery." Alex sipped from his beer, but he didn't move. "I'm glad you came."

"Really?" The word flew from her mouth and she instantly felt her cheeks heat. "I mean, thank you."

A smile turned up the corners of Alex's mouth. "I also want to apologize again for what happened last week, and say I'm sorry I made things strange between us over dinner."

Now her heart raced. "You thought things were strange between us?"

"Awkward."

When he said the word she laughed. "That's what I told Rachel. That it was awkward."

Now he chuckled. "It shouldn't be. We've been friends for a long time."

"You're right. And I don't blame you for what happened last week."

"Good. Did you get the job?"

"No."

He nodded slowly. "That's too bad. I hope your black eyes didn't have anything to do with that." She shrugged and sipped her wine again.

Alex bit down on his lip. "I'd like to take you out to dinner, try it again?"

She took another sip of her wine and gave it some thought. With Rachel married now, she didn't really have anyone to spend time with. Would it be so bad if two old acquaintances finally got to know one another?

"Okay."

"Okay?" His smile was wide now. "Wednesday?"

She steadied her breath, because she thought she might hyperventilate. "Wednesday would be fine."

"It's a date, again." He turned a put his arm around her shoulders. "Rachel looks miserable," he said as they started toward the back yard.

25

"It's ninety degrees."

"And you look beautiful in your sundress," he said very casually. Before she could say *thank you* for the compliment, he opened the back gate. "Ray wants to talk to you, by the way." He waved toward Ray who was throwing bean bags at a board in the yard. "Hey, Ray, she's here."

As all eyes turned toward her, she suddenly wished she'd stayed in the car and driven away.

"Awesome," Ray said as he handed Craig his pile of bean bags. He walked over to Catherine, kissed her on the cheek, then stood back to look at her. "You look lovely."

"Thank you," she managed this time.

"I hear you're looking for a new job."

She didn't know what she'd expected him to say, but she wasn't sure that had been it. "I am."

"I need an office manager," he said and Catherine felt her eyes widen.

"For construction?" She wasn't even sure she was right, was that what he did?

"Yeah. It's a solid forty hours, or more sometimes. I need data entry, filing, phone answering, email writing." He took a breath. "You're completely over qualified for the job, but…"

"But it sounds like just what I need right now," she said smiling up at him. "I'd love to discuss it with you."

"Great. If you're open to stop by tomorrow, I'll text you the address."

"I can be there."

"Perfect."

Catherine smiled. Now she was glad she got out of the car.

CHAPTER 7

*S*iri announced that Catherine's destination was on the right. She passed the long fence with the name of the company on a banner. *Stewart Builders* welcomed her with another sign on the gate, so she drove through.

In the center of the lot was what she would consider a temporary building, but it had been there long enough it had established landscaping around it.

Catherine parked near the entrance in one of the designated visitor parking spaces. She recognized Ray's truck, even without the designated parking sign stating that it was his.

Stepping out onto the gravel, she quickly realized that her choice of footwear needed to be rethought. This wasn't a high rise, in fact, looking around, she didn't quite know what to make of the empty lot.

She closed the door to her car and noticed Ray standing on the front step of the building with the door open.

"C'mon, I have air conditioning in here," he said.

Catherine closed the door and headed up the little walk and into the air conditioned building.

She couldn't help but smile when she walked inside. The little yard outside was cute, but the building gave no hint to what was inside.

Had she not just walked in from a gravel path, she would have thought she'd walked off the elevator into company headquarters on the thirtieth floor.

A wall met her with bright silver letters that said *Stewart Builders* and a young man sat behind a reception desk, that had obviously been custom made. To her right she saw two offices with nameplates on the doors, and to her left was a conference room behind a glass wall.

"This is gorgeous," she said to Ray as he closed the door and stood next to her.

"You have to make a good first impression. This is Allen, he runs our reception."

The young man, perhaps twenty, stood and shook Catherine's hand.

"It's nice to meet you. Catherine Anderson."

"Can I get you anything, Ms. Anderson?" Allen asked. "It's hot out. We have ice water and lemonade."

"Ice water would be fantastic. Thank you."

She watched as Allen walked around the fancy wall and disappeared.

"C'mon, let me introduce you to my temp," Ray said, smiling.

He knocked on the office door, even though it was open and Catherine watched as the woman behind the desk rose.

"Catherine, this is my mother, Clara."

Before Catherine could extend her hand, the woman wearing a cardigan, embellished with a large floral pin, pulled her in and hugged her.

"It is so nice to meet you," she said, still gripping Catherine's arms. "Ray could use some good help. He says you're over quali-fied." She scanned a look over her. "Over dressed too. You will want to keep the nice clothes for nice events."

"Thank you," Catherine managed.

Ray chuckled. "Mom has been helping out, but you might gather she's a little anxious to get out of here."

Clara nudged her son. "I've been retired for years. This has been nice, but I'm missing lounging at the pool with my friends," she admitted with a wink. "You two go discuss details and let me finish my work."

"It was nice to meet you," Catherine said before they left the room.

"You too, honey," she called out as they walked to the other office.

"She'll be disappointed if you don't take the job," Ray said closing the door behind them, and Catherine noticed there were two glasses of ice water at the small table in the office. "Let's sit here. It's more casual."

Catherine took the seat Ray offered her and sat down. He sat down across from her and immediately took a sip of his water.

"Not much more to see on the tour. Two offices, conference room, kitchenette and bathrooms in the back. Everything that has to be done is basic organization, and knowledge of the industry will come. I spend my day between here and building sites. I do most of the coordinating of sub-contractors, but I would love, if you take the job, for you to get to know that side too. It would really help me out."

"Ray, I know nothing about construction."

"Neither does Mom, but I'm always a call away. Allen knows a lot, and really, I just need someone who can say 'let me find out for you,' and call people back with the answer. You have no idea how much that would take off my plate. I know you have the skills. You're organized and personable. I think you're the right fit."

Catherine picked up her water and sipped. She considered that this might have been the longest conversation she'd ever had with Ray one on one. Did he really see something in her, or was he that desperate?

Who was she really to question that? She was that desperate.

"And how often does this office move?" she asked looking around.

Ray narrowed his eyes. "What do you mean?"

"I mean you have a temporary building fenced in on a prime Denver lot. I assume this is a future Stewart build."

Ray ran his hand over the whiskers on his chin. "Right. Well, this is a high rise apartment building that never was. I bought the land to build my own concept, but the financial backers backed out. So, it became headquarters. Someday, maybe it'll be what I imagined, but for now, it's an eyesore in the center of town."

"Then they should come inside. It's amazing what you've done with it."

"I appreciate that. So what do you think? I know I'm just dumping a lot of stuff on you with not a lot of explanation. I'm hoping you remember me as someone who was a swell guy and you might take a chance on." His eyes grew wide then. "I mean in business."

Catherine contained her grin. "Under one condition. If I'm not doing the job right or well, you have to tell me. You have to either then educate me or kick me to the curb. I don't want special treatment, but I do need the job."

Now Ray smiled. "I promise to give you the tools and teach you everything you need to know."

"Then I accept your position." She held out her hand to him.

Ray shook her hand and held it for a moment. "Alex was right, you're pretty amazing."

CHAPTER 8

*a*lex pressed the button on his steering wheel to connect his hands free speaker to answer his phone.

"Hey, Ray!" He said loudly, making sure Ray heard him.

"Just called to say thanks, buddy."

Ray chuckled. "And what did I do?"

"Catherine. She's going to work out perfect for the job."

Alex eased to a stop at the light. "You hired her?"

"I didn't really give her a chance to say no. Seriously, I need her. Rachel told me what she did for the district, so she's completely over qualified for what she's going to be doing. But she needs the work."

"She needs the change of scenery," Alex said as the light changed and he eased through the intersection.

"Something happened at her last job?"

"Rachel got shot," he reminded Ray. "She wants something she can just walk away from at the end of the day."

"I didn't think about that," Ray admitted.

"That's why I thought she'd be good for the job. Well, that and the fact that she has all the skills."

"She starts tomorrow."

That brought a smile to Alex's face. At the next intersection, he turned right to head back out of town.

～

CATHERINE BLEW A STRAY HAIR FROM HER FACE AS SHE STOOD BACK and examined the paint color on the wall of her tiny guest bathroom. One thing about a new build, the primary color throughout the house was white, and that was needing to change.

Because it had been years since she'd decorated and painted a room, she'd decided to start in the guest bathroom.

Home Depot had gladly taken her money for the new mirror, paint, back splash tile, and a rug for in front of the vanity. The warm brown was going to make the tiny room a cozy place for guests to visit.

Knowing she was heading to a new job in the morning, she'd wanted to get as much of the painting done as possible. She pulled her phone from the pocket of her paint stained overalls and looked at the time. It was nearly six.

Catherine looked around the small room. It was possible she could have the painting done by nine. The rest could wait for the weekend.

Just as she carried her tray of paint up the ladder and secured it, her doorbell rang. She bit down on her lip.

She wasn't expecting anyone. Stepping down off the ladder, she took her rag from her pocket and wiped her hands. No need to carry paint throughout the house.

The accent windows next to the door were clear, and she could see a man on the step, his back toward the door as if he were looking at the construction that surrounded her. Next on her list was to get blinds for those windows, or some kind of decorative coating so people couldn't see right into her house.

Catherine opened the door slightly and Alex turned toward her, a bouquet of flowers and a bottle of wine in his hands.

"Hi," she said, still hiding behind the door as if he were some solicitor.

"Hey." He smiled and lifted his sunglasses to the top of his head. Those dark eyes met hers and she swore she felt just a little light headed. It must be the fumes, she decided as she opened the door a little wider.

"What are you doing here? We did say Wednesday, right?"

His smile widened. "We did. But I talked to Ray and he's over the moon that you took that job, so I thought a celebration was in order. I brought flowers, wine, and I'm fairly handy with a paint brush."

"What?"

He scanned a purposeful look over her and she looked down at her paint covered overalls.

"Oh," she laughed. "I was painting the guest bathroom."

"I can bring all of this back on Wednesday, if it would be better."

Catherine realized he was still on the front step and she hadn't invited him in. "No, you can come in. Sorry." Alex stepped inside. "I was trying to get the bathroom painted tonight. I hadn't expected to have a job to go to in the morning when I'd planned this."

Alex held out the flowers and the wine to her. "My gym bag is in the car. I can change and help. Seriously, I'm at your service if you'd like."

And did she like? She looked down at the flowers and the wine. "Ray said you told him I'd be good for the job."

"I did tell him that. He had mentioned that he needed someone, and after our discussion the other night, I knew you'd be right for it."

Catherine chewed her bottom lip. "That was very nice of you."

"What are friends for, right?"

Friends. No longer just acquaintances, but friends. "I appreciate it. Are you sure you want to paint?"

Alex stepped in closer to her, pulled the rag from her pocket, and gently wiped her cheek with it. "You had a little on you. Brown?"

Her breath caught in her lungs having him that close. "Yeah."

"Nice." He kept the rag in his hand. "I'll get some different clothes. I'll be right back in."

Catherine stood in the doorway watching him walk down the steps to his car. She let out that breath that had stuck in her chest. *What are friends for, right?* The words played over in her head.

She blinked hard and forced herself to turn from the door. Friends were for having one another's backs, for celebrating little wins like new jobs, and for picking up paint brushes. Friends were there when other friends were traumatized and they rallied.

Catherine carried the flowers and the wine to the kitchen and set them on the counter. Friends didn't make your insides twist up and your skin flush.

Maybe that was a side effect from coming to consider Alex Burke a friend. She'd had plenty of years where the mention of his name made her insides tense not twist.

She heard him close the front door, and that caused her heart rate to ramp up. Maybe she was having an allergic reaction to him, she thought and chuckled to herself.

"What's so funny?" his voice came from behind her.

"Nothing. Nothing at all."

CHAPTER 9

"Where can I change?" Alex asked as he watched Catherine unbundle the flowers and cut the ends off the stems before putting them into a vase.

"Straight up the stairs is another bathroom," she said without ever turning around.

Alex took her direction and headed up the stairs. No wonder she was painting, he thought. Every wall was contractor white at the moment.

The bathroom was at the top of the stairs, just as she'd said. He stepped into the room, stark white as well, accented only with a beige, linen shower curtain, and brown rugs on the floor. Obviously she was going for earthy tones. He shut the door, and thought there must be one more bathroom. He wasn't sure the bathroom he stood in had ever been used.

Alex slipped into a T-Shirt and a pair of shorts. He folded up his pants and shirt, then opening the door, he stepped out and looked around.

There were two bedrooms upstairs. The one to his right was small enough, he knew it must be a spare room, but he could only see a desk situated under the window. Down the hall was another room, but the door was partially closed.

There was a little part of him that wanted to open the door and see what the room told him about her, but he wasn't that kind of guy. He wouldn't go in until he was invited.

That thought shook him. Did he want to be invited?

He considered it. Catherine Anderson had always held his interest, probably because she was anything but interested. Didn't that always make someone more appealing? However, she'd been around him for months now, and she seemed comfortable enough to accept invites when they'd have dinners and barbecues. And didn't he think of her right away when Ray said he needed someone for that job? Then, when she got the job, hadn't he headed straight to her house to celebrate?

Shit! Maybe he did want an invitation.

Alex walked back down the stairs, laying his clothes by the front door.

Catherine wasn't in the kitchen when he returned, but he heard the distinct sound of a roller full of paint on a wall. He walked toward the bathroom and saw her standing on a ladder.

"I could do that for you. You won't have to reach as far," he said as she looked down at him.

"I feel bad that you're going to help at all."

"I love feeling useful."

She studied him for a moment before she stepped off the ladder. "If you do the walls I can do the edging."

"Sounds like a plan."

In the confines of the small room, they inched past one another, careful to not touch. Alex started up the ladder and Catherine picked up a brush and began to go around the trim of the door.

A bit later she disappeared, and he heard Eddie Van Halen's guitar wail from the other room, and then the volume increased.

"Is that okay?" Catherine asked as she walked back into the bathroom.

"Can't go wrong with Van Halen. David or Sammy?" he asked, and Catherine wrinkled her nose.

"Each have merit. My mom was a fan of David's long hair. But, I'll admit, I liked Sammy better."

Alex chuckled. "Me too."

They continued their painting as the playlist moved from Van Halen, to Queen, to Backstreet Boys, and then to Sinatra.

"You have eclectic music taste," Alex said as he moved the ladder slightly.

"I had older influences. My brother and sister are ten years older than I am. It influenced what I listened to. Likewise, my parents were older, so I cross many generations."

"I like it." Alex finished the section of the wall as the music changed again to some hair band ballad he didn't even remember the words to.

He stepped off the ladder and looked at his work. It wasn't bad. Catherine finished the section she was working on and stepped back to look. But in the confines of the bathroom, she stepped back into him.

Instinct had his hands coming to her waist to stop her from going back further.

"Sorry," she said.

"Don't be. Do you dance?"

Spinning to face him, the paint brush still in her hand, she looked up at him, now that they were toe to toe.

"What?"

Alex took the brush from her and set it on top of the open can of paint. "Do you dance?"

Now he wrapped his arms around her waist and pulled her closer. Her eyes were wide as she studied him. She might have thought he was crazy, but she wasn't pushing him away.

A few measures later, she finally lifted her arms and swayed with him.

"This is silly," she chuckled shaking her head.

"Spontaneous," he corrected as he pulled her a little closer. "It's supposed to be romantic, right? Stopping what you're doing and dancing?"

Her eyes went wide. "Are you trying to be romantic?"

"Am I not good at it?"

Catherine blinked and he could see her lip tremble. "I asked you first," she said and her voice shook.

Alex slowed his sway. Maybe he was trying to be romantic. Maybe that was why he felt the need to show up at her house with flowers and wine.

He slowed even more, until they were simply standing in the bathroom—his hands on her hips, her arms around his neck.

"I guess I am," he said looking down into her blue eyes.

Catherine swallowed hard and ran her tongue across her pink lips. "Then I guess you're good at it."

The ball was back in his court, he decided. He could let go of her and pick up the paint roller, or he could take the next step and see what happened.

Catherine's fingers began to make circles at the nape of his neck, and now he trembled.

Lowering his mouth, until his was only a breath from hers, he stopped and locked eyes with her. Her baby blues were soft before they disappeared behind her eyelids, and he knew then she wanted the kiss he was contemplating as much as he did.

Alex closed the gap between their lips, and felt Catherine's body ease against him as his mouth opened to hers. He moved Catherine to the doorjamb and pressed her back against it as her fingers tangled in his hair.

This certainly had taken their acquaintance and friendship to another level, he thought as he cupped her bottom in his hands and she let out a moan. What the hell was he doing getting involved with her? His luck never panned out well with women, and this woman was too entwined in his life. The best friend of one of his best friend's wives. Could it get more complicated?

When Catherine's hands came to his chest and eased him back, he opened his eyes. Her blue eyes had gone nearly gray now and she bit down on her lip. "I think we'd better think this through," she said on a heavy breath.

Yeah, they were on the same page.

CHAPTER 10

*I*t hadn't surprised Alex when the text message had come through earlier in the day.

Something came up. I need a raincheck on dinner. ~ Catherine

As he sat in the back yard, beer in his hand, and sun setting over the Rockies, he read the text again.

It wouldn't have been the first time he'd misread a situation with a woman. He thought back to when he'd met Cara after moving to Boston. They'd misstepped at least ten times before they decided they wanted to be a couple. Oh, the wining and dining, that too, he remembered. Then it was hot and heavy. She moved in, and it was normal. They lived together well.

In the mornings she'd start the coffee, he'd wash their mugs before he left for work. They met at the gym in the afternoons, cooked dinner together, and relaxed on the couch to watch TV until they crawled into bed.

They'd had a routine. He supposed he'd been so smitten with her, and their routine, he didn't even notice when routine turned into excuses. *I have to work late. I have a meeting. The girls are going out for drinks. I need to borrow some money.*

Alex took a long pull from his beer. What a freaking idiot he'd been.

"I thought you had a date," Bruce said as he walked out of the house, a beer in his hand.

Like other nights, he carried a chair out into the yard, and sat on it backward to watch the sunset with Alex.

"She backed out," he said.

"Ouch."

"Yeah. I'm thinking she still isn't interested in me."

Bruce took a pull from his beer. "I don't actually buy that. Playing hard to get?"

"No." Alex raked his fingers through his hair. "I kissed her," he admitted and Bruce lowered his beer before taking another drink.

"When?"

"Monday night. I took flowers and wine over to celebrate with her, and we kissed."

"You started it?"

Alex had to think about it. "I think I did."

"You think."

"Man, we were both into it."

Bruce lifted his beer to his lips and took a long sip. "Maybe she just needs time. Ya know, she had Rach to herself all these years. Coach dies, we all decide to stay in touch, Rach marries Craig, and now we're a permanent fixture in her life. Too much too soon?"

"Maybe. I guess I'll see how she reacts the next time we see each other."

Bruce stood and picked up the chair. "I think if you're really interested, it'll work out. I see how she looks at you."

Alex laughed. "And how is that?"

Bruce walked toward the house, setting the chair down near the patio table, and then opening the back door. "She longingly looks at you the same way your sister looks at me," he said on a laugh that came from his belly.

As Alex spun to look at him, he let the door close, but he could still hear him laughing.

Alex shook his head. Bruce would be a dead man if he ever touched Alex's sister, and Bruce knew that. And didn't he have a lot of fun with it?

Easing back in his chair, he watched the last bit of orange succumb to the top of the mountain, and disappear.

Alex finished his beer in the darkness now, and stilled to listen to the city around him.

It wouldn't be long before he and Catherine were around each other again. But he didn't really want to wait too long.

He picked up his phone and scrolled through his contacts until he reached Ray's.

Food trucks are at Civic Center Park tomorrow. I'm buying. He texted and waited for the reply that came almost immediately,

I never can turn that down. Meet you there?

Alex quickly replied. *I'll park in your lot. We can walk over.*

As he finished his beer, Ray's text came back. *See you then.*

Standing from his chair, he grinned to himself. Okay, now they'd see how she reacted when Alex walked through the door of the office tomorrow.

WHEN THE DOOR TO THE OFFICE OPENED, CATHERINE WATCHED Allen's head lift and a smile form on his lips.

"How can I help you?" he asked.

"I'm here to pick up Ray for lunch," she heard the voice of the man that had walked in.

Cranking her head slightly, she saw Alex walking toward the front desk. He was casually dressed in a pair of jeans with a dark colored polo shirt.

"Mr. Stewart is on a conference call. Can I get you something to drink?"

Alex shook his head, and turned to see her staring at him from behind her desk.

"No. If you don't mind I'll wait for him. I'll go talk to Catherine until he's ready."

Her eyes opened as wide as Allen's had when he strolled into her office.

"Nice digs," he said looking around.

She noticed the moment he'd seen the flowers he'd brought her in celebration sitting on the file cabinet.

"Thank you," Catherine said. "You're going to lunch with Ray?"

"Food trucks at Civic Center. We've tried to go a few times this summer. Usually one of us is busy, but..."

"You're not working today?"

"I'm lucky enough to set my own schedule. I can work remote when I want, stay late when I need, and have greasy food truck food with friends, whenever."

"That sounds really nice," she said with her voice quivering.

He didn't seem as awkward around her as she felt around him. Perhaps pushing back from that kiss had been the right choice.

Ray walked in behind Alex. "Hey, I'm so sorry I didn't call you. I'm on the phone with a subcontractor and I'm going to be a bit. Why don't you go without me?"

"It's no big deal," Alex said. "I get it."

Ray nodded. "Why don't you take Catherine?" He turned to face her. "Take as long as you like. Seriously, you've done in two days what would have taken my mother a week to do. But don't ever tell her I said that. I think she did it that way so I'd replace her."

"Oh, I don't..."

"No. I mean it. You should go with Alex."

Alex's brows rose. "What do you say? Can I buy you lunch?"

Before she could agree, or not, Ray put his hand on Alex's shoulder. "Don't hurry back, but bring me something. If it has pork, I'll be super happy."

He laughed as he left the room, and Alex smiled at her. "Well, let's have lunch."

CHAPTER 11

*C*atherine had quickly learned to wear sensible shoes and clothes to the office, and now that she was walking, in the sweltering heat, she was glad she had.

She'd shrugged off her light sweater, which she wore under the air conditioning, and the sun beat down on her bare shoulders. Alex walked next to her as if the heat wasn't getting to him, his hands tucked into the pockets of his jeans.

"You really don't have to take me to lunch with you. I packed…"

"Save it for dinner," he said turning to her and smiling. "This is nice."

They walked three more blocks in silence and the heat on the back of Catherine's neck, under her hair, was nearly unbearable.

She opened her purse, which she wore across her body, and took out a hair tie. In a well-practiced move, she gathered up her hair and knotted it on the top of her head, fully aware that Alex had watched her every move.

"I like your hair like that," he said.

"Thank you?" She wasn't sure what to make of it.

"It accentuates your neck and now I can see those little earrings you're wearing."

Catherine reached her hand up to touch the small hoops that dangled from her ears. "Rachel gave these to me when she got married. A thank you gift for always having her back."

"I don't know anyone who's had someone's back more," he agreed. "You're a good friend."

She let that resonate for a moment. After last night, she didn't even feel worthy of friendship.

They stopped with a crowd at the light and waited for the walk signal. The park was on the other side of the street, and food trucks lined its walkway.

Catherine turned and looked up at Alex. He was so casual standing among the others that surrounded them. He had an ease to him, as if nothing ever bothered him. How was that? How did someone stay so cool and collected all the time?

When he looked down at her, through dark sunglasses, he smiled. "What's on your mind?"

And what could she tell him? '*You*'?

"I'm sorry about last night," she finally said, as if her conscience decided what to say before she had.

"No sweat. Some other time. This was a nice bonus," he said as the light signaled that the crowd could walk.

When they made it to the other side of the street, the crowd went in different directions, and she followed Alex toward the row of trucks.

"Sky's the limit," he said. "Pizza, gyros, fish tacos, regular tacos."

Suddenly she wasn't sure she could stomach anything. "You pick."

"There's a barbecue truck on the end. We'll get something there and pick up something with pork for Ray."

They walked through those who stood and studied the menus, and headed to the barbecue truck. Because she couldn't decide, he ordered them each pulled pork sandwiches, and one to go.

When he retrieved them from the window, he looked around. "I don't see any table space, but there's shade under the trees. Should we picnic?"

Shade sounded good.

Catherine followed him away from the crowd to a group of trees at the corner of the park. They sat down on the soft grass and leaned their backs against the tree as they opened their bags of chips, bottles of water, and sandwiches—which Catherine knew she'd be taking most of back with her.

Alex bit into his sandwich and let out a low hum. "This is good."

She pulled a piece of the pork from between the sliced roll and took a bite. With a nod, she agreed.

Sipping his water, Alex shifted so that he was turned in her direction.

"Listen, I'm sorry about the other day. I shouldn't have shown up unannounced and stayed. I overstepped the line."

He was apologizing. Catherine had to process that. Did he really have anything to apologize for? She invited him in. She let him stay. She ran her damn fingers through his hair and pressed herself up against his firm body.

Her body temperature rose just thinking of it.

"There's nothing to be sorry for. I was as much a part of that as you were."

A smile curled his lips. "You're not sorry?"

Catherine let out a breath. "I don't know what I am. Confused, mostly."

Alex chuckled. "Because we kissed and you don't like me."

She felt her eyes go wide and her mouth opened as if she were surprised to hear him say that, but why wouldn't he say that, or think it? She'd spent her time around him making sure he understood her disgust with him. God, talk about holding a grudge.

47

She'd probably led him on when she'd spent time at his house when Rachel and Craig were dating.

The quick assessment of what she was feeling spun in her head. Alex Burke wasn't the enemy, and she knew it. She'd made him the enemy when he turned to Rachel instead of her all those years ago.

Catherine nearly choked on her breath when she realized it. It wasn't that she didn't like Alex, though she thought he was a bit of a player when she was younger. But the biggest problem with her assessment of him then was that he wasn't interested in high school girls, back when she was interested in him. He looked right past her, and hadn't she always had eyes for him? Then, when he did come around, he went right to Rachel.

God, thinking about it was making her sick.

She opened her water and took a long sip to ease the discomfort in her chest.

When she'd settled, she looked at him sitting casually eating his lunch.

"I do like you," she said and Alex lifted a brow, as if he'd forgotten the last thing he said. "I've never been very nice to you though."

Alex picked up his napkin and wiped his mouth. "That's a lot to take in."

Now her hands shook, so she capped the water and sat it on the ground. "I was never nice to any of you. You buzzed around Rachel and her family like a swarm of bees. I get it," she said holding her hand up to ward off any comments. "Mr. Diaz set it up that way. Having you all around kept you mostly out of trouble. But it distracted her, and that took her mind off of being *my* friend. It's petty, stupid, and small of me. But, hey, I was a teenage girl."

Alex pulled his sunglasses from his face and hooked them on the front of his shirt. "And now? All these years later, we're swarming again?"

"Yes," she said breathlessly. "But I'm not sixteen anymore."

Resting his hand on the ground, he eased toward her. "So you don't hate me?"

Catherine swallowed hard. "I don't think I do."

"You're not mad about what happened the other night?"

"Mad, no. Conflicted, yes."

He smiled again as he inched closer to her. "You're more comfortable hating me."

"I never actually hated you."

"You didn't?"

"You didn't see me, that's all."

Humor flashed in his eyes. "Oh, hell, you have no idea, do you?"

Catherine eased back. "What does that mean?"

"It means let's discuss that over dinner. No backing out, okay?"

She nodded as he gazed into her eyes.

CHAPTER 12

*T*hey walked back to the office in near silence. Catherine had a conversation going on in her own head, she was surprised she even remembered he was walking next to her.

As they walked toward the building, the gravel crunching under their feet, Alex reached for Catherine's arm and pulled her toward him. He handed her the bag with Ray's sandwich.

"I'll come to get you at six," he said inching closer to her.

"Okay," her voice shook as she spoke. "I'll be ready."

Inching even closer, he wrapped an arm around her waist. "By the way, I noticed you," he said softly before pressing a gentle kiss to her lips, which had her head swimming in the heat.

He stepped back and walked toward his car.

"Don't you want to say goodbye to Ray?"

Alex shook his head. "Nah. I'll catch him later."

He gave her a wave, climbed into his car, and a moment later drove away.

It took her two full breaths to settle herself after he'd kissed her.

He'd noticed, he said. He'd seen her all those years ago.

Catherine needed to decide how she was going to handle all of this.

With Ray's lunch in her hand, she walked through the front door of the office. Ray sat behind the desk, where Allen usually sat.

"I have your lunch," she said handing him the bag. "Where is Allen?"

"Lunch."

"And now you're doing his job?"

Ray shook his head. "Just fielding a few phone calls," he said looking up at her and smiling. "Nice lunch?"

"It was fine."

He raised a brow. "Fine?"

"Yes."

"And you and Alex?"

She crossed her arms in front of her. "What are you really asking?"

Ray stood and walked around the reception desk, leaning against it as he stood in front of her. "I saw you just now. When did that start?"

"It didn't start."

"It didn't look like a friendly goodbye. It looked a little more involved."

Catherine unfolded her arms and wrung her hands together. "I don't know what's going on there. I'm conflicted—a lot."

Ray smiled and reached a hand to touch her arm. "If it's any help, he's a great guy." He winked and walked back around the reception desk, picked up his lunch, and headed to his office.

Catherine stood in the reception area, her hands shaking. What was she supposed to do?

Whenever she'd needed anything, she'd turned to Rachel. Was that a wise choice now?

The phone rang, and she snapped herself out of her thoughts.

She had a job to do. She could worry about falling for Alex Burke later.

As Catherine drove out of town, the traffic slowing down her drive, her phone rang, and she answered it with her hands free button on her steering wheel.

Before she even got the word *hello* out of her mouth, Rachel's voice screeched through the speakers of her car.

"You said it was awkward. What in the hell are you doing kissing Alex Burke?"

Catherine gritted her teeth. That information could only have been passed to Rachel by one other person, okay two, but for some reason she didn't think Alex was a kiss and tell kind of guy.

"It was awkward," she confirmed.

"But now you're kissing him in public?"

"Are you accusing me?"

"I'm asking," Rachel confirmed. "C'mon, it's the middle of August. I'm already uncomfortable. I feel as if I'm the size of a house, and I hardly even show. And I'm only going to get bigger. Let me live vicariously through you."

"You have a good love life."

Rachel giggled. "I do. God, I do."

"I don't want specifics," Catherine warned.

"But, c'mon. You and Alex, what's going on?"

Catherine decided to avoid the highway, and headed toward the next main street. Something told her she needed to take the long route home.

"I don't know what's going on. He showed up on Monday night to celebrate me getting the job with Ray. He brought wine and flowers."

"That's romantic."

"Well, I was painting the bathroom. So, he changed and

decided to help. Nothing much to think about, really. We didn't even open the wine. But one thing led to another and..."

"Oh, my God! You slept with Alex."

"Get your head out of the gutter. When have I ever just jumped into bed with someone?"

Rachel laughed and it echoed through the car. "You should. You're due."

Catherine let out a breath. "I didn't sleep with him. But, we kissed."

Rachel eked out another squeal. "You kissed Alex."

"We kissed each other."

"That's what I mean. And now you're together?"

Catherine turned at the light and continued on as the traffic thinned out. "We're not together. We decided we needed to think about it and discuss it."

"I'm confused," Rachel said. "You kissed him at your house, and again today."

"And who told you that?"

There was silence for a moment. "My husband."

"And where did he hear it?"

"Ray," Rachel confirmed softly.

That's what Catherine thought. Wasn't this one of the reasons you didn't get involved in a group of friends? Then again, she chuckled to herself, wasn't it kind of endearing at the same time?

"He came to take Ray to lunch. Ray couldn't go, so I went. We talked about me not liking him, he apologized for the kiss on Monday. Somewhere I said something about being petty and jealous that they were always around you and your family, and I wasn't noticed at all."

"Oh," Rachel's word was soft. "Is that how you felt?"

"Rach, I don't want to discuss that."

"Seriously."

Catherine pulled over into a grocery store parking lot and parked her car. "They were always around, the guys. You and your brothers had this wonderful and changing family year to year. This group of guys just happened to come along when we finally noticed them—you know, as men." She rested her head against the headrest. "Alex never paid me any attention, and then when Craig disappeared after graduation, Alex was knocking on your door. I think I took that personally."

"Cath, you never said anything."

"You went away. I went to college. The guys all disappeared. I had you to myself for the next decade. No man ever came along that disrupted our friendship, until Craig came back."

"Our friendship is intact."

Catherine laughed. "I know. I told you it was petty."

"You should come over and let's sit and talk about this."

"Rach, there's nothing to talk about. Besides, he's picking me up at six for dinner. I backed out on Wednesday when we were going to go out again."

"To make up for the awkward?"

"Yeah."

"He's a good guy, Cath. A really good guy," Rachel said vouching for Alex, just as Ray had.

"I think I'm ready to believe it."

CHAPTER 13

*C*atherine had changed her clothes four times. She'd gone from a cute sundress to a jumpsuit that covered every inch of her body. Next came the pair of distressed jeans and a T-shirt, and she was back to the sundress.

Standing in front of the full length mirror in her bedroom, she played with her hair. Should she put it up? Should she let it fall? Was she trying too hard?

With a grunt, she grabbed the jeans and the T-shirt and changed out of the dress again.

By the time she was done, she was in a pair of sandals, with the jeans and a button down, sleeveless shirt. She'd pulled back her hair and added a pair of earrings that dangled from her earlobes, which Rachel and her mother had given her when she'd graduated college.

Just as she'd reconsidered the attire one more time, she heard the sound of a car door.

Catherine moved to the window to see Alex walking up toward her door with what looked like a cake box, and another bottle of wine. She was going to have enough wine stockpiled to have a cellar.

Deciding that she was dressed now, and that was as good as it was going to get, she hurried down the stairs and pulled open the door just as Alex lifted his finger to ring the bell.

"I saw you coming," Catherine said breathlessly.

"You look beautiful."

She looked down at her outfit, having forgotten what she'd finally settled on to wear. "Thanks. Come in."

As he stepped through the door, he held out the box in his hands. "Are you up for a change of plans? My mom has a friend who has a dinner service company, and they were making grazing boxes. I picked her up one, and thought it would be a fun dinner for us. But, with that said, I'm totally okay to go out too."

Catherine took the box. "I don't even know what this is."

"Wait till you see it."

She looked at the bottle of wine in his hand. "We never opened the bottle you brought on Monday," she reminded him.

"Gives me a reason to keep coming back," he said, a smile curling up the corner of his mouth.

Catherine knew she was in dangerous territory if she wasn't willing to gamble a little with her heart.

Walking toward the kitchen, she took the opportunity to settle her breath. She set the box on the table and realized that Alex wasn't with her. A moment later he walked from the bathroom.

"It looks nice. We did a good job."

That caused Catherine to laugh. "We did."

Alex set the bottle of wine on the table. "Seriously, though, we could go out. You do look really nice."

"Full disclosure, I changed four times."

"I'd love to see the other choices." That charming smile was back, and for a moment she considered his comment.

"I'm good with staying in." She lifted the lid on the box and let out a little gasp. "Oh my, look at all of this."

The box was filled with meats and cheeses. There were crackers, olives, grapes, nuts, and even candies.

"Is this goat cheese with blueberries?" she asked.

"Looks like it."

"This is almost too pretty to eat," she said picking up a grape and popping it into her mouth. "It's still hot out, and they're working and kicking up dirt. However, this is too fun to sit at the table." She looked up into his dark eyes. "What about a picnic on the coffee table. We can sit on the floor, have our wine, and enjoy this for dinner."

"I think that sounds amazing."

HAD A BOX OF CUTE FOOD OFFERINGS ACTUALLY CALMED HER around him, Alex wondered. He wasn't going to overthink it. At the moment she didn't have that invisible wall up around her. Something had changed since he'd left her after lunch.

Catherine took two wine glasses from the cupboard, pulled a couple sheets of paper towel from the roll, opened a drawer and took out a corkscrew, and picked up the bottle of wine.

"C'mon, there has to be a Marvel movie on TV we can watch while we indulge in this," she said with a casual laugh.

Alex watched her walk out of the kitchen. Oh, he'd noticed her all those years ago. Now, here she was, comfortable in her own home, and it was twisting him up.

This was a completely different side to the anxious woman he'd taken to lunch.

He picked up the box and followed her to the living room. She'd set the glasses and napkins on the coffee table. With the bottle still in her hand, she picked up the remote control, and then sat on the floor, her back pressed against the sofa.

Looking up at him, she batted those long lashes. "Do you want to open the wine?"

Alex set the box on the table, and took the bottle of wine

when she handed it to him with the corkscrew. As Catherine surfed through the TV channels, Alex pulled the cork from the bottle.

"Iron Man 3?" she asked, looking up at him.

"I can't compete with Tony Stark," he teased, setting the bottle on the table and sitting down on the floor next to her.

"Oh, I don't know about that." Catherine picked up the wine and studied the label, he assumed to avoid eye contact after that comment. "One of Toby's?"

"Yeah, he set me up nicely."

Catherine poured them each a glass of wine, and then handed him a glass. "We need a toast."

"Do we?"

"Don't we?" She bit down on her lip and his body temperature rose a few degrees.

Alex held his glass to hers. "Here's to it not being awkward."

Her lashes batted again and he saw the pink rise in her cheeks. "Cheers to that," she said softly as she lifted the glass to her lips and sipped.

Alex did the same, but now their eyes had locked. Something between them had escalated in the few hours they'd been apart. What had been an unfortunate accident, turned into an awkward dinner, accentuated by an impromptu drop by and a heated kiss. And somehow an intimate lunch and a kiss goodbye had prompted her to compliment him with Tony Stark comparisons and now had a civil manner toward him.

Lowering his glass, Alex kept his eyes on hers. Her cheeks were even pinker after drinking the wine.

Catherine lowered her glass and flicked her tongue across her lips, which twisted him up. She set her glass on the table, and turned her head casually toward him.

"It's okay," she said softly, gazing at him.

"What's okay?"

"It's okay to kiss me again."

58

CHAPTER 14

*N*ever in his entire life had Alex thought so hard about a kiss. Kissing was natural, instinctive, and often impromptu, like the two kisses they had already shared. This one, the one that hadn't happened yet, but was causing his brain to freeze up, was important.

Well, hell, they were all important, but what kind of kiss was he supposed to plant on those full, pink lips?

Did she expect him to gently press a kiss to her mouth and then pull back, as he had at lunch? Or should he assume she wanted the heat of the kiss from Monday night, where he'd pressed her up against the doorjamb and her fingers had tangled in his hair?

Her lashes batted again and he watched as she eased away from him. The moment had gone.

"It's okay," she said. "I think I misread the situation."

"I don't think you did."

She picked up a grape, held it to her mouth, and then lowered it. "I'm not good at this stuff. The dating, or the figuring it out, or even the kissing." She popped the grape into her mouth. "I guess I thought…"

He waited for her to continue, but she'd gone silent.

"You thought what?"

When she looked back up at him, her eyes had gone damp. "I thought you might be interested in me."

They were going to have this conversation again? "I don't think you misread the situation at all. I think I was overthinking it."

"Are you interested?"

"Remember when I told you I'd noticed, I meant it. I've been interested since the day I met you," he admitted as he set his glass on the table. "I was very much under the impression you weren't interested in me."

Catherine bit down on her lip. "I'm interested."

Lifting his hand to her cheek, he held her eyes with his. "This could get complicated."

"I'm fully aware of that. I've already had phone calls."

Alex eased back a bit, keeping his hand on her face. "Rachel?"

"Ray talked to Craig, and so on, and so on."

Alex chuckled. "Okay, then let's make a pact. It doesn't get complicated."

"How do we avoid that?"

"We follow the momentum, and never let it get that way," he said as he closed the gap, taking her mouth with his, and swallowing the sigh she let out as she lifted her arms and wrapped them around his neck.

The heat of August had nothing on the heat they created just by pressing their mouths to one another's. Her tongue met his, and he thought he might have forgotten how to breathe.

In a fluid motion, he lowered her under him, pinned between the coffee table and the sofa. Their mouths still connected in a maddening kiss that had kick started his entire body into gear.

When he pressed himself to her, she'd moaned and wrapped her legs around him tightly. Still fully clothed, he'd never felt an energy like the one buzzing through him with anyone else.

Bracing himself with one arm, his mouth still working against hers, he cupped her breast in his hand, and she pulled back.

Alex removed his hand, and opened his eyes to meet her shocked stare. "I'm sorry. I thought…"

"It just took me by surprise. That's all." Taking his hand, she placed it back on her body, but he felt her fingers tremble against his skin. "It's okay."

"Are you sure?"

Catherine lifted her mouth back to his. "I'm sure," she whispered against his lips.

HER EYES CLOSED AND SHE SQUEEZED THEM TIGHTER WHEN HIS hand came to her breast again. There was no reason for her to flinch at his touch. It was incredible to have him that close to her, let alone touching her.

Catherine felt him between her legs. His thumb rubbed lazy circles against her nipple, through her clothing, and heat sizzled over her skin.

She'd had this dream in high school, she'd remembered. Alex Burke moving on top of her, making her feel things she'd never felt before. But the dream had been whisked away when she'd watched him move in on other girls. Every party she'd seen him at, he'd left with a girl. Catherine was invisible.

She squeezed her eyes shut harder. That was the Alex of the past—wasn't it, not the man who rocked against her, who had her heart rate racing and her breath clogged in her lungs… he wasn't that same man.

He'd noticed her. Maybe it had been her that hid the entire time—afraid of being caught and hurt.

Alex's lips broke from hers and moved down her neck. Catherine sucked in as much air as she could, because she was finding it harder and harder to breathe.

She wanted this. She'd always wanted this.

Alex moved his hand to the buttons on her shirt, and nimbly, began to unbutton them single handedly. As each button opened, he pressed a kiss to her skin. And each time his lips skimmed over her, Catherine let out a small gasp.

"You're beautiful," he whispered into the crook of her neck. "You've always been so beautiful."

"Alex…"

He pressed his forehead to hers. "I'm not going to not say it." His lips skimmed over her collarbone. "I've dreamed of this, Catherine."

Alex eased back and looked down at her.

"Tell me you've thought of this too," he urged, nipping her lips with a kiss again.

The answer on the tip of her tongue felt hypocritical. But they were being honest. "It was all I thought about in high school."

Now Alex hovered over her. His eyes wide.

"Seriously?"

"Don't tease me," she pleaded.

"God, no. I'm not teasing you."

"Rachel had eyes for Craig, but my eyes were on you."

Alex rose up on his knees and looked down at her. He blew out a breath and scanned a look over her laying beneath him, her shirt open, exposing her to him.

"I wish I had known that."

"What would it have changed? You would have had to wait for me, just as Craig waited for Rachel," she said and then reconsidered. "Or she waited for him."

"I would have."

Catherine rose on her elbows and shook her head. "I don't think you would have. Maybe we need more time for this."

Alex cupped her face with his hands. "This is just a lot to take in. We lost so many years."

"I think we're right where we're supposed to be." Catherine gathered the front of his shirt in one hand and lowered him back down on top of her. "All those years ago, it wouldn't have worked." She steadied her breath as she rested her head to the floor. "Kiss me some more. Then we'll drink the wine, eat the food, and you have to go. But for now, continue to kiss me senseless."

CHAPTER 15

*C*atherine yawned at her desk, picked up her coffee, and took a long sip, though it had gone cold.

Many things had changed over the past decade. Staying up until the wee hours of the morning making out with a man took its toll on a grown woman. At least if they'd had sex, they might have ended up in bed at a reasonable hour and gotten some sleep.

"Everything okay?" Allen's head came around her partially closed door and he smiled.

"Long night."

"We have a subcontractor meeting in the conference room in twenty. Ray wants you to sit in. We have them every Friday morning. You'll want to add that to your agenda."

Catherine blew out a breath. "I think I'm going to need more coffee for that."

Allen gave her a wink and disappeared.

She considered what she needed to take with her to the meeting. Perhaps just a notepad and a pen, she thought as she looked over her desk. She supposed if she needed anything else it would be right across the room, basically.

As she added the meeting to her agenda, and clicked the repeat button to schedule the meeting weekly, her phone buzzed.

Rachel's name flashed on the screen. *I'm hungry for nachos. Girls' night tonight?*

Catherine studied the text as she eased back in her seat.

Her entire life had been about accepting these kinds of invitations, and making these kinds of plans herself. For the first time in forever, her fingers didn't automatically slide across the screen and confirm. Her mind went directly to Alex. The need to see him jumbled her brain.

They were adults. Making out wasn't going to hold them off for long, she thought. The next time they were together, it could be the opportunity they would take to move this *thing* they were exploring to the next level.

Catherine's palms grew damp.

It was exactly what she wanted, but she found that it created a new anxiety she hadn't dealt with in years—years.

It had been so long since she'd been with a man, she wondered if a person could earn back their virginity.

The thought made her chuckle, and her phone buzzed again.

The guys all have plans tonight to get together. Just in case that matters, Rachel's text read and Catherine smiled.

Picking up her phone, Catherine confirmed girls' night and nachos. Perhaps a night away from the man that made Catherine's insides sizzle would be a good thing. It would give her more time to consider her next move.

ALEX PULLED INTO THE MASSIVE DRIVE IN FRONT OF TOBY'S HOUSE. He was the last one to arrive. They'd all parked in the driveway, and still there was plenty of room for even more cars.

As Alex stepped out of his car, he looked up at the house. It was a sight. Its rugged Colorado architecture with wood accents and large windows welcomed those who visited.

Walking to the front door, Alex wondered just how lonely it would be to drive up that driveway after work, without another car parked there. Was it refreshing to walk through the front door after a long day and hear your footsteps echo? He couldn't imagine.

There hadn't been a lot of time in Alex's life when he didn't live with someone. Even once he'd moved back to Colorado, Bruce was in the basement when he'd bought the house from Craig. Back in Boston, he'd only been alone a few months once Cara finally made her exit. It sure had made the decision to move back easier.

No, he couldn't imagine that walking into the monstrosity of a house like Toby's would give him any comfort.

He rang the doorbell and waited. There was humor in the fact that it took nearly a minute for someone to reach the front door.

When the door opened, it was Craig standing on the other side with a margarita in his hand.

"Welcome, my friend," Craig said smiling.

"We're having margaritas?"

"We're having tequila. This is the form I chose to drink mine. Bruce and Ray have chosen salt and lime."

Alex laughed as he stepped through the door and followed Craig through the house to the staircase the led them to the walkout basement where Toby had a fully stocked bar, stools, an enormous TV, pool table, dart board, and of course four full sized arcade games.

Bruce and Ray held up their empty shot glasses, letting out a *whoop* when they saw Alex walk through the door. This was one of those nights he knew they'd all wake up on the sofa, or in one of the large reclining chairs that faced that huge TV.

His thoughts went directly to Catherine and how much he wanted to see her. Was a night with his friends what he wanted?

Hell, he needed that more than anything. But there was a deep-seated need to be wrapped in her arms too.

"How are you taking your tequila?" Toby asked from behind the bar.

Alex moved to the bar and rested his arms atop of it. "Is that really my only choice?"

"This is product testing. I have an option to buy in."

Alex laughed and shook his head. "I'll take one of those shots, as long as we're not taking body shots off each other."

The comment caused Bruce and Ray to laugh, and Toby refilled their shot glasses.

Alex moved in next to Bruce and Ray. He quickly counted the number of chewed up limes in the little bowl, and decided they'd had a head start on him. Chances were they would be staying the night.

Bruce mumbled something about a countdown, and passed the salt shaker to Alex, who childishly licked his hand, sprinkled salt on area, and picked up his glass.

"One. Two," Bruce's words already slurred. "Now!"

The three of them licked the salt from their hands, drank down the shot, then picked up a wedge of lime and sucked on it.

Alex laughed at the antics, and felt a peace being around his dearest friends. In that moment, he missed Coach, but was so grateful for the man, that even in death he'd brought the five of them back together. Their brotherhood was solid.

Alex looked into his empty shot glass. "It's smooth."

"Nice, huh?" Toby lifted the bottle to pour him another shot, but Alex warded it off with his hand.

"Maybe a beer?"

"Sure."

"But, in all honesty, it's good stuff. I think you should invest."

Toby laughed. "I did."

CHAPTER 16

*R*achel was already at a table, the platter of nachos before her, when Catherine arrived.

She hurried through the noisy bar and wrapped an arm around Rachel's shoulder, then planted a noisy kiss on her cheek.

"I'm sorry I'm late. My mother called," she said as she hopped up onto the tall stool across from Rachel.

"How is she?"

"Old enough that she can't hear when I tell her that I'm headed out. She just kept talking and talking." Catherine laughed. "I'm grateful. My parents can't hear a word I say, but they're both around to annoy me."

Rachel nodded. "I can confirm that you're right to be grateful." She took a chip and bit down on it. "I still find myself, six months later, wanting to call my dad, especially when all the guys are around. They'll bring up some memory, and I want to share it with him."

"I'll bet that's hard."

"Considering everything that has happened in my life in the past six months, it's just something else I have to process. Thank goodness for a good therapist."

Rachel said the words with humor, and Catherine believed that's how she viewed it—with a sense of humor. Since February, Rachel's father had died, she fell in love with—or rekindled the love that had been there for—Craig, gotten pregnant, and been shot. That was enough to make anyone a little punchy, but Rachel took it in stride.

Catherine studied her dearest friend in the world. She wore a tank top, which she wouldn't have done even a year ago. The sleeve tattoo on her arm was bright and beautiful, covering up scars that told a different story.

The scar on her shoulder, peeking from under the fabric of her shirt when Rachel moved, was from where a bullet had entered her body, and Catherine knew on the back side, there was a matching scar from where the bullet exited. Of course there were numerous other scars from where they'd done surgery to repair Rachel's shoulder. She favored it now, Catherine knew. Even long after the baby was born, Rachel would still be recovering in many ways.

"You didn't have other plans tonight, did you?" Rachel asked, stirring Catherine from her thoughts.

Picking up a chip, Catherine shook her head. "Nope. Free as a bird."

"Uh-huh." Rachel grinned. "Do I have to pull every word of this story out of you?"

"What story?"

"You and Alex."

"What's to tell?"

Rachel picked up her water with a slice of lemon, and drank it from the straw. "You said you were going to have dinner last night. Did you? Was it awkward? Did you kiss him? Did you sleep with him? Are we planning another wedding?"

Catherine felt her mouth fall open. "Are you kidding me with all of this?"

"I need gossip. Please," Rachel pleaded with a smile as she set down her water and picked up another chip.

Catherine blew out a breath to steady herself. "He came over. We ate at home. Drank wine, and," she closed her eyes, "made out all night long."

Rachel let out a giggle and tapped her finger tips together. "You made out?"

"First base. Second base. We might have even approached third." Now Catherine laughed. "I don't want to gossip about this."

"It's not gossip. You're sharing details with your very best friend."

"Who is married to one of Alex's best friends."

Rachel shrugged. "It keeps it nice and tidy." She leaned in on her elbows. "And you're here with me. Alex is with the guys, so no home run tonight."

Catherine felt her head spin. "I don't even want to think about it."

"I do."

"Do you know how long it's been since I've been with a man? Seriously, that night at Alex's when I fell asleep on the couch with my head on Toby's shoulder, that's the most action I've had in forever."

Rachel gave her a considerate thought. "That's sad."

"I've always been gun shy."

"Because of what? You're a hot commodity," Rachel said.

"It has nothing to do with my body. I saw what getting your heart broke did to you. What if that happened to me?"

Rachel reached for her hand. "God, you're giving me lots to talk to my therapist about. I'm so sorry."

Catherine shook her head. "No. Don't be sorry." She let out another breath. "He broke my heart when he came for you all those years ago. He didn't know it. You didn't know it. It's so petty it makes me sick."

"But you've been in relationships."

Catherine raised her brows. "A relationship. One."

"That was like four years ago."

"I know. That's part of my angst."

Rachel sat back in her chair and rested her hands on her stomach. "You haven't had sex in four years?" She gave it more thought. "Dear, God! You were in that relationship all through college. That's the only one? The only guy?"

"Don't look so shocked."

"I can't help it. Why didn't I know this?"

"Because we never had reason to talk about it. This changes everything."

"You've been on dates since then."

Catherine took another chip and bit down on it. "Dates. All dates don't end in sex."

"They should," Rachel argued and that caused Catherine to laugh.

"I'm not as confident as you are."

"And now you're going to have sex with Alex Burke?"

The thought of it made Catherine nearly snort out another laugh. "About time," she said and even Rachel laughed now. "He's the only person I've ever wanted to have sex with. I mean, you know, fantasized about." Catherine felt the heat in her cheeks when she admitted that out loud.

"Then it's a lucky coincidence that he came back when he did. God, you might turn into some kind of prune otherwise."

Catherine thought that this was what made their relationship so wonderful. They could talk like this and neither one judged the other one.

Rachel leaned in and took another chip, letting the cheese string from the plate to her mouth, then gathered up the cheese with her finger and placed it on the chip. "He's a good guy, but I've said that before."

"You have. So did Ray." Catherine leaned in. "Tell me, it's okay though. I mean, you and Alex…"

"Shared some kisses. Maybe we got to second base too," she chuckled. "He was there to support me as a friend. And I was a really messed up friend at that time. Don't hold it against him. You might miss out on something really wonderful if you do."

Catherine nodded. It wasn't about the sex, it was about the feelings that had been building up inside of her since she was fifteen. She had the opportunity to make Alex Burke hers, and that was exactly what she wanted.

*a*s predicted, Bruce and Ray were passed out on the sofa. Craig had left nearly two hours earlier to go home to his wife.

Toby sipped a beer at his bar, his feet propped up on one of the other bar stools.

Alex threw darts at the board and nursed a bottle of water.

"I can't decide if I should go get pillows and blankets for these losers, or just let them wake up as they are," Toby humored himself watching Ray and Bruce.

"Leave them. It isn't the first time. It won't be the last," Alex said as he walked toward the board and retrieved the darts.

"Your mind is extremely occupied," Toby said finishing off his beer. "Need an ear?"

Alex stood back and aimed the dart at the board. "Catherine Anderson," he said as he released the dart.

"I heard something about that. What about her?"

"There are some very strong feelings buzzing between us. They stem from teenage years, but shit, they're still buzzing."

Toby laughed and lowered his feet. Standing, he stretched. "Not sure what to do about that?"

"I'm very sure what to do about it. I just think I need to handle her differently. Besides, I'm still a little hurt from the last woman who had me buzzing."

"What was her name?"

"Cara," Alex bit the name out as he aimed and threw the next dart.

"We're all allowed one major screw up."

"Yeah, well I didn't know it was a screw up." He turned and faced Toby. "Six. Six different guys," he said, shaking his head. "How the hell do you think something is perfect and your girlfriend has six different affairs?"

"Shit."

"Yeah, shit."

Toby walked around the bar, dropped his bottle in the recycle, and turned off the lights that illuminated behind the bar. "That's not Catherine."

"Yeah, well I don't want to be the guy on a rebound either."

"How long has it been since you've seen Cara?"

Alex blew out a breath. "Ten months or so. She was moved out before I came for Coach's funeral."

"It sounds like you've had plenty of time to rebound. This is something else," Toby assured him. "What this is, is a long time coming."

"It gets complicated if someone gets hurt."

Toby nodded his head. "Someone is going to get hurt. Someone always gets hurt. It's how you deal with it."

Alex laughed, threw the last dart, and then tucked his hands into his front pockets. "How did you get so wise, hermit in a big house?"

"I'm not always alone. I'm just saying. We're all adults. We can all handle a few pushes and shoves. Tell her how you feel. Work through the shit. Get over Cara and move on."

"I'm over Cara," he said sternly.

"Then there isn't a problem. I think there will be a bigger problem when Bruce finally gets to your sister."

Alex felt the blood drain from his face, but when Toby laughed, he knew it had been said for the purpose of making him mad.

"That was a shit move."

Toby moved to him and put his hand on Alex's shoulder. "Admit it. She could do worse."

Alex didn't want to admit it. He didn't want to think about his sister and any of his friends.

CATHERINE TOSSED IN HER BED. THE AIR OUTSIDE WAS STILL AND the fan did nothing to cool her. She'd save for air conditioning the next summer. Seriously, a new build that cost that much should just come with air conditioning. But she was glad to have the house, so she wasn't going to complain. If all else failed, she'd go to the basement and sleep there.

But it wasn't just the heat in the room that was keeping her awake. Alex was on her mind.

They'd had a few texts between them all day, but was she already expecting more? It had been an amazing night with Rachel, and she was sure he'd had a good time at Toby's. That would still always be the case, even if they did start a relationship.

She pounded her pillow into place again, and readjusted just as her phone chimed.

Who in the hell was texting her at midnight?

Then panic zipped through her. God, hopefully nothing had happened with her parents.

She rolled to the edge of the bed and picked up her cell phone from the charger.

There was immense relief when she saw Alex's name on the screen.

Sorry it's so late. You're on my mind. Are you up?

Catherine let out a small laugh. *I'm awake. I can't seem to sleep.*

A moment later she heard the door bell and she sat up with a start. Seriously? He was there?

Kicking off the sheet, she dropped her feet to the floor, and hurried toward the door. Half way down the stairs she realized she was in a very revealing tank top. Her nipples pressed against the fabric. Maybe she'd better go put on a bra or a sweatshirt. God, no, she'd die in a sweatshirt.

Hell, the man had already touched her and seen her. The heat rose in her body just thinking about him touching her.

What was a skimpy pair of shorts and a tank top going to hide now. She didn't even want it to hide anything, and wasn't that some of the aggravation she was having with herself?

Catherine hit the light at the bottom of the landing, and she could see him through the window, his hands propped up on both sides of the door.

When she disabled the alarm, unlocked the door, and pulled it open, he was right there.

"Hi," she said breathlessly looking up at him.

"I had to come," he said.

"I'm glad you did."

Catherine stepped back and Alex walked through the door, closing and locking it behind him.

He turned and scanned a look over her, and she fought every instinct to not cover her body.

Alex's hands came to her hips and he pushed her back against the wall and took her mouth with his. The room grew even hotter she thought as he pressed himself against her and she felt him.

This was it. There was need and hunger. Alex lifted her to his hips, grinding against her, and she wrapped her legs around him.

"I don't want to stop," he said as he brushed his mouth over her throat.

"I don't want you to stop."

"If we do this, it starts something," he said as he pressed his forehead to hers.

"We've already started it."

CHAPTER 18

*H*er worry over the tank top was only a memory now, as Alex's hand slid under the fabric, and brushed over her breast. With his mouth on hers, Catherine fought for breath, and then devoured his kiss as if it were life.

With her still wrapped around him, Alex managed to get them both to the top of the stairs.

"Corner bedroom," Catherine said, her words muffled against his neck.

He walked down the hall to her room, carefully maneuvering them through the door, and then lowered her to the bed.

This was the moment she'd fantasized about since she was a teenager. Only, over the years, the fantasy became more involved, but this was where it would start.

Alex looked down at her, the moonlight illuminated her body, but she didn't cover it. The heat she fretted over earlier was even warmer now, but she just didn't care.

He gathered the hem of the tank top and pulled it over her head, then he lowered his mouth and feasted on her sensitive skin. Catherine closed her eyes and let every sensation he brought to her wash over her as she arched against him.

Catherine tugged at his shirt until she had pulled it over his head. Now his skin pressed to hers, heightening the sensations that blurred her vision.

She slipped her hands between them and worked on the button of his pants, while he shimmied the shorts from her hips with his hands. Then, quickly, he managed to discard his pants, all the while engaged in the life-giving kiss that Catherine knew she couldn't live without.

Their mouths worked together as hands roamed over naked bodies. Every thought Catherine had ever had about that very moment was exploding in her mind. Alex Burke was in her bed, naked, with his body on top of hers. There was a crash to be had, she was damn sure of it. But at that moment, she was higher than she'd ever been.

Alex rolled her onto the bed fully, her body pressed beneath his. Their skin was already damp with sweat from the heat of the room and the intensity of the kisses and touches they'd splayed over one another. As she wrapped her legs around him and he pressed against her, she eased him back with her hands on his chest as her mind became fully aware of the situation they were in.

"Wait," Catherine sucked in a breath. "Condom."

Alex's eyes went wide, and he leaned back. "Tell me you have a box in the drawer," he bent to kiss her mouth before she answered.

"No. Shit!" she bit out the word as he eased back. "I didn't expect this. I'm not covered. Do you have some in your car?"

Alex rose up on his knees and looked down at her. A smile formed on his lips and then he let out a chuckle as he lowered himself to lay next to her, propping himself up on an elbow, and resting his other hand on her stomach.

She wondered if he could feel the jitters that bounced around inside of her when he touched her so intimately.

"Let's just say, I haven't seen the need to have any in my

immediate possession since I moved back. And, I didn't know this was where I was going to land tonight," he said as he took Catherine's hand and interlaced their fingers.

Catherine bit down on her bottom lip. "I haven't had sex in four years," the words tumbled from her mouth and she wondered if he would laugh or leave.

"Four years? That's an extremely long time."

"I don't sleep around."

Alex leaned in and placed a gentle kiss to her lips. "That bodes well for me, considering my last relationship."

Swallowing hard, Catherine looked up into his eyes. "I'm sorry someone did that to you."

"I've been known to not be a great judge of character." He ran his thumb over her knuckles. "I don't think that's the case now."

"This took the night in a different direction," Catherine said as she rolled to face him, cupping his face in her hands. "Full disclosure, because I feel as if I owe it to you, especially now that I seem to have put a damper on things." She searched his eyes for something that said he was disappointed, but she didn't find it. "I've only been with one other man. I've only been in one relationship, and that was over four years ago. I don't have a lot of experience, obviously. I'm not on the pill. I don't have condoms."

Alex pressed a kiss to her lips. "I never assume the woman should take care of all of that. Just so you know. And, in full disclosure, I've been with more than one other woman."

"I knew that." She brushed his hair from his forehead. "I used to watch you leave parties with girls. I knew."

Alex winced. "I'm a bit disgusted by my actions back then, especially now."

"I always thought you were a player. I know that was some of my attitude toward you. But it never stopped me from watching though."

He ran his hand over her hair. "I wish I'd known you were watching." Alex let out a slow breath. "Do you eat donuts?"

The question caused her to laugh. "What do donuts have to do with contraception and sexual partners?"

"Everything really."

"Yes. I eat donuts."

Alex pulled her in closer to him and kissed her thoroughly. "I'm staying the night," he said without discussion. "I'm going to sleep right here with you in my arms, just like this. When I wake up, I'm going to go get donuts and a big box of condoms."

Catherine laughed again. "A big box?"

"I think we're going to need them. You don't have any plans for the day do you?"

"None."

"Then consider the rest of your day booked. No need to even get dressed."

CHAPTER 19

*C*atherine felt the breeze blow through the open window and heard the birds singing their morning songs. She rolled and opened her eyes to find her bed empty.

She looked down at her naked body, and knew it hadn't been a dream. Alex had been there.

Picking up her phone from the nightstand, she looked at the time. Six-thirty. For a moment she listened to the sounds, wondering if he'd just gone to the bathroom or was downstairs, but she heard nothing.

Sitting up, she looked around the room. His clothes were gone, but hers had been folded and placed on the end of the bed.

Catherine pulled on the tank top and shorts Alex had taken off her in the wee hours of the morning. Standing, she pulled up the sheets on the bed, and went to find him.

It wasn't until she hit the bottom of the stairs that she smelled the coffee brewing. She stopped for a moment to collect herself. Alex Burke had slept in her bed, wrapped his arms around her, and hadn't had sex with her. Catherine pressed her hands to her nervous stomach.

But sex with Alex was on the agenda for the day, she knew —all day.

He was seated at the table, a cup of coffee in front of him, and a box of donuts in the center of the table. Cautiously, Catherine looked around the room for the other items he'd said he was going to buy.

"They're in my car," he said looking up at her.

She felt the heat rise in her cheeks. "Oh." Feeling the need, she folded her arms in front of her, as if to cover herself. "You've already left and come back then?"

"I didn't want to miss a minute." Alex stood and moved to her, gathering her in his arms, and she wrapped hers around his neck. "I left them in the car, because we have a lot to think about."

"We do?"

Alex pressed a kiss to her lips. "I've known you since you were fourteen. I've learned that I made quite a fool of myself in front of you," he admitted, and pressed a finger to her lips when she took a breath to argue. "A lot happened to both of us in the ten years since we saw one another. And now, I've seen you every week, but this," he kissed her again, "this is new."

Running her fingers into his hair, she gazed into his dark eyes. "What are you trying to tell me?"

"I'm trying to tell you that I think we should date."

Catherine laughed. "Isn't that what we're doing?"

His hands moved from her hips to cup her bottom. "We're skipping from friendship to lovers. I think we need to take a moment to collect ourselves."

"And how long will that take?" she asked, hoping it didn't sound desperate.

"I don't know. Let's spend the day together. Let's run errands, have lunch in some crowded center, and tomorrow go to the YMCA for basketball, hand in hand."

"You want to present us in public? Is that what you mean?"

"I guess it is. I know everyone is on our side, and I know they all know, but let's make it official, before we make it *official*."

Catherine bit down on her lip. "I don't know if I want to wait any longer."

Alex lifted his hand to her cheek. "After what you told me last night, I want to make everything special for you. You deserve something better than me showing up in the middle of the night and ripping off your clothes."

Catherine laughed. "I rather enjoyed that."

"So did I. But let me woo you," he said before he gently kissed her. "Let me make you fall in love with me."

"Wow," Catherine let the word out on a breath. "You have some mighty big goals."

"Like I said. You deserve better, and shit, if you're going to settle for me, I'd better be the best."

When he said that, she felt the tears begin to sting her eyes and she batted them before her eyes welled with them. "I already happen to think you're the best. And Rachel and your friends tend to back up that notion."

"I'm glad to hear that. Now sit down. I'll get you some coffee, we'll eat donuts, and then go walk around a home improvement center," he teased and she laughed. "We'll be normal in public, holding hands."

How could she possibly turn that down?

AFTER LUNCH, WHICH THEY'D PURCHASED FROM A LOCAL DELI AND eaten in the center of a pedestrian mall, they did just as he'd suggested, and roamed the aisles of Home Depot.

Alex had humored himself by buying a toothbrush holder for her bathroom sink. He then promised he was going to keep a toothbrush at her place.

With her fingers intertwined with his, she laughed. "I'll clear out a drawer for you to put some of your things in."

And that, he thought, was almost more intimate than sex.

They stopped by his house to pick up a few things, including his gym bag for the next morning. As he packed his duffle bag, he thought about the condoms he had in his night stand. He supposed it was a staple, though he'd long ago stopped carrying them in his wallet.

He heard Catherine moving about in the other room, and he considered snatching her up and off her feet, and depositing her right there on his bed. Bruce wasn't home. It would be spontaneous and intimate—and protected.

Chuckling to himself, he shook his head and zipped up his bag.

His misguided lust was what had him abstaining from having sex with Catherine in the first place. He wanted it to be more. He wanted to make love to her when it was time. It needed to be more than just sex for the sake of sex.

"Your plant in the living room needs water," her voice came from the doorway, and Alex lifted his head to look at her.

"I have a plant in the living room?"

She laughed easily. "Well, I don't know if you could call it that anymore." Catherine moved to him, pressing her hands to his chest, and lifting on her toes to kiss him. "We could stay here tonight, if you want."

"No, Bruce will be home at some point."

"Right. Roommates always make it awkward to walk around naked in the kitchen."

Alex felt his stomach tighten. She was going to need to fall in love with him soon, He wasn't sure how much longer he was going to last at holding her off.

CHAPTER 20

*C*atherine unbuckled her seatbelt and watched as their friends began to walk through the parking lot to the entrance of the YMCA.

She hadn't been there to watch one of their friendly games since Alex had given her two black eyes. Laughing she opened the door and stepped out as Alex pulled his bag from the back.

"Will I need protective gear today?" She asked as she shut the door and walked to the back of the car.

Alex laughed. "I want to say you won't be a distraction to me today, but you might be more of one." He wrapped an arm around her waist and pulled her to him, placing a kiss on her mouth. "God, that's what you are. You're my distraction."

She smiled, but she wasn't sure if that was a compliment. Considering he said it and then kissed her, she was going to assume he meant it as one.

Alex closed the back of the car, picked up the gym bag, and took hold of Catherine's hand as they began to walk toward the door.

"I was thinking of getting some steaks tonight and grilling.

Would you be interested? Bruce said he was going to make some kind of pasta salad."

"I don't want to get in between roomies and their dinner."

Alex slowed. "It's casual. Don't think you'll ever come between me and my friends. It's all new again anyways, isn't it? I told them they were stupid for not having hung out for the last decade. Coach brought us all together again. I'm extremely thankful for that." He looked down at her. "Friends are important. I know that. So let's just make this clear now. I enjoy your company, and you are part of my friend group, but I will never ask you to sideline other relationships you have, like with friends."

"That happened to you, didn't it?" she asked, realizing they still had a lot to learn about one another.

"Cara wasn't fond of boys' night out. I guess that should have been my clue when she started going out with her girlfriends," he said adding a set of air quotes with his free hand.

"Rachel is my only friend. We do nachos and margaritas often, more so when she's not pregnant," Catherine laughed. "I appreciate our time."

"Then always make sure you take that time."

Catherine stopped, and Alex turned to her. "Let's just get this out of the way."

"Okay," he said slowly.

"We're dating."

A small smile turned up the corners of his mouth. "I think we'd agree on that."

"We're a couple. Alex and Catherine. Catherine and Alex."

"Catchy either way."

"I've seen you naked."

Now his smile was wide as he gathered her up with one of his arms. "And I've seen you naked. And I like it."

"I appreciate that too. What I want you to know is that I will never lie to you," she promised. "I will never cheat. If I say I'm fine, give me a little space, and then ask again, because I'm probably not fine. But the space will be appreciated. My family is very important to me. I will choose them over you."

"As you should."

"My friends are important to me."

"Understood."

"I don't know what our future holds, but someday I'd like to get married and I'm not so old that I've ruled out not having kids. I still want to have kids."

"Okay."

"The only relationship I was ever in, it obviously didn't go the way of marriage and kids. We wanted different aspects of being a couple. So we parted."

Alex lifted his hand to her cheek. "I'm not opposed to marriage. I was raised in a good one. I just figured I'd never have kids because I hadn't found their perfect mother in my mate." He smiled down, gazing into her eyes. "If you are that perfect mate, it would be exactly what I'd want too."

Catherine swallowed hard. "But this is new."

"It is new, and we're about to introduce it to our friends."

"They'll all be happy for us."

Alex nodded. "Of course they will. They all like you, and I know they'd like me to be with someone who is good to me—and them."

She laughed. "Okay." She let out a breath. "I just thought we should clear up those few things."

THEY WALKED THROUGH THE DOOR AND INTO THE GYM, HAND IN hand, just as Alex had wanted to.

Bruce greeted them with a quick nod and went back to lacing up his shoes. Ray smiled and gave Catherine a wink.

Craig looked up from his seat on the bench next to Rachel and smiled. "Catherine, don't you have any taste?" he teased.

It wasn't until Toby and Sarah walked through the door that Alex got a reaction from anyone.

Still holding Catherine's hand, he nipped her lips with a kiss and heard his sister's gasp.

Toby turned to Sarah as they neared Alex and Catherine.

"This is news to you?" Toby asked.

"I guess it is," Sarah said looking at Catherine. "Don't you have any taste?"

Craig threw up his arms. "That's what I said."

Catherine sat down next to Rachel, who nudged her with a smile.

Alex sat down on the other bench next to his sister and pulled his shoes from his bag.

"So when did this happen?" Sarah asked in a hushed tone.

"Fourteen years ago."

Sarah's eyes grew wide. "What?"

Alex chuckled. "We've just had eyes on each other that long. But the official us, it's new."

"I'm happy for you. I'm concerned for her," she teased. "Seriously? She couldn't do better?"

"Some people just stick things like this out."

"If you're lucky she will. To be honest, I didn't think she liked you at all."

Alex puckered his lips. "I may have jeopardized a few morals in her book. But, I've grown up a bit. I've been traumatized by a woman. And now I'm surrounded by good people. That seems to give me some cred."

"She's good people," Sarah agreed as she finished tying her shoes. "But just because you're in love, I'm not going to go easy on you. I'm here to kick your ass."

Alex laughed again. He wouldn't have it any other way.

CHAPTER 21

For the next week, they had dinners together, and slept in their own beds after heated kisses goodnight. But, they'd both agreed, if they were waiting out sex, they should at least go home at night.

Though Catherine was about done waiting.

She was new to the relationship game. The one she'd had was not stellar, though it lasted for years. I love yous had been shared, and meant, back then. But since then, she hadn't given herself, or her feelings to anyone else.

Now there was Alex, and the words and the actions all belonged to him, but how was she supposed to be the one to say it? The ball was in her court and she knew it. But if she said it, was she just saying it to move things forward? Would she mean it if she said it? She felt it.

She pressed a hand to her jittery stomach.

Every morning in the shower she played the words and scenarios over in her head. Should she text him? Call him? Say it while they were kissing?

Maybe she never should have told him that she'd gone years

without sex and had only had one other partner. Maybe the condom wasn't that big of a deal that night.

She cursed herself as she stood in front of the mirror and blow dried her hair.

When her phone buzzed, she looked down to see Alex's name on the screen.

"Hello, handsome," she said as she answered his call.

"Good morning, beautiful. Rachel and Craig want to head downtown to Union Station for dinner. Are you in?"

Double dating with her best friend was certainly a perk when dating the friend's husband's best friend. At least it had become a positive twist to the negativity she'd given the idea a month ago.

"I think that sounds like fun," she agreed.

"I'll come by and pick you up around five. By the way, after that, you're coming home with me," he said without asking. "Pack a bag."

Catherine sucked in a breath and bit down on her lip. Perhaps he was tired of waiting too.

"I'll see you in a little bit," he said before they disconnected the call.

Catherine looked in the mirror again, her cheeks now pinked. Tonight. She was going to tell Alex Burke she loved him tonight.

AT FIVE O'CLOCK, ON THE DOT, THE DOORBELL RANG AND Catherine set down the kitchen towel in her hand and walked to the door. When she pulled it open, Alex stood there holding a pot filled with petunias.

Catherine smiled. "What is this?"

"I thought your back patio needed a little color. I know you're waiting to plant things until the construction around you is done. But, still, you should have some color."

Catherine laughed as she stepped aside to let Alex through. "That was very thoughtful of you."

"Not really," he admitted. "My sister's office was selling them as a fundraiser for one of her co-workers who has a kid in the hospital. I bought a pot for my back yard, your back yard, my mother's back yard, and I donated to the cause monetarily too."

And didn't that just make Catherine's heart tumble?

"That was very generous of you."

"I lost my dad to cancer. I can't imagine having a kid with it."

Catherine swallowed hard. "That's what the fundraiser was for?"

He nodded. "Yeah. I don't think me buying flowers is enough, but it's what I could do in the moment."

Catherine could feel the tears stinging her eyes and she batted them back, but he'd noticed.

Alex set the pot by the door and gathered her in his arms. "I didn't mean to upset you."

"Upset me? How do you think you upset me?"

He wiped away a tear that escaped and rolled down her cheek. "You're crying."

"Because what you did was moving. On all levels. The gift to me. The sincerity with which you contributed to that family."

"We're not all dealt the perfect hand in life. It's the job of those of us who have had it better to help those who need it."

And there, her heart tumbled again. She never would have assumed that the Alex Burke of her past would be the man in front of her, though she should have known that was who he was deep down. The reason she'd had problems with him for all those years stemmed from his generosity and kindness, didn't it? Hadn't he come to help Rachel through a hard time? Though it might have been shrouded with bouts of lust and misunderstanding, that had been his mission through it all.

"I love you." The words had fallen from her lips as she looked up into his dark eyes, which gazed down into hers and made her head swim.

Alex's eyes went wide and a smile formed on his lips. "You love me?"

Catherine let out a breath and a nervous giggle. "I guess I do. It just came out."

"Those are some big words."

"You're not teasing me are you?"

He shook his head. "Oh, hell no. I'm taking it in. Say it again."

Catherine studied him for a moment, before licking her lips to moisten them. "I love you."

Alex cupped her face in his hands. His eyes had gone darker now. "No one has ever said that to me."

Now her eyes went wide. "You were in a relationship for a long time. You lived with…"

"With someone who was self-centered and took and took. Catherine, no one has ever looked me in the eye and said those words to me."

"I'm your first?"

He chuckled at that. "In so many ways. Say it again."

Now she laughed. "I love you, Alex Burke."

Alex lowered his lips to hers and pressed a warm gentle kiss to them. Then lingering there, just a breath away, still holding her face in his hands he whispered, "I love you too, Catherine."

CHAPTER 22

*C*atherine's insides buzzed through dinner, as if she had a secret she couldn't keep much longer. When Rachel excused herself from the table to go to the restroom, Catherine did the same and walked with her.

"Seriously, the bigger this baby gets, the more time I spend in bathrooms," Rachel laughed as she pushed open the door and hurried into the first stall.

Catherine stood at the sinks and looked at her face in the mirror. How could the whole world not know what she'd said to Alex a few hours earlier. The grin on her face nearly spelled it out.

When the toilet flushed and Rachel exited her stall, Catherine took her lipstick from her purse and glided it over her lips.

"I told him I love him," she let the words fall, much as she had when she told them to Alex.

With her hands still under the water, Rachel looked at her in the mirror. "You told Alex you love him?"

Catherine put the lid back on the tube of lipstick and nodded. "It just came out. That has to be the right time then, right? When the words happen spontaneously?" Now she was second guessing it. "Right?"

Rachel laughed as she pulled her hands from the water, which then shut off, and walked toward the paper towel dispenser. "I just didn't see this coming." She wiped off her hands and threw the paper away. Then she ran her hands over her stomach. "Well, I didn't see any of this coming."

"I'm happy," Catherine admitted. "I do love him."

"He's a good man."

"So you've said."

"He deserves a good woman."

"I'm scared to death."

Rachel moved to her and took her hands in hers. "If the words *I love you* rolled off your tongue, then I'd say you mean them. When too much thought is put into it, I think it can be contrived."

"Am I ready for this?"

Rachel laughed. "Ready or not, here it is. But no one deserves it more, Cath. I'm very happy for you. Enjoy this. Don't overthink it."

AFTER DINNER, THEY SAID THEIR GOODBYES, AND ALEX HELD Catherine's hand as they walked to the car. There wasn't much to say, he was simply enjoying the feel of her hand in his and the closeness.

When they got to the car, he opened the door for her and let her climb in before skirting the front of the car, opening his door, and sliding in.

"I've never eaten there before," he said as he started the engine. "It was nice."

"It was nice. And I swear, Rachel gets bigger every time I see her," Catherine said, resting her head back against the seat. "I have never seen her so happy."

"She deserves it, after everything she's gone through."

Catherine nodded. "She's still going through it, but I think this helps."

"She's doing okay though, isn't she?" He turned to look at her briefly before focusing back on the road.

"She has nightmares," Catherine confirmed. "She still sees a therapist, and so does Craig so that he can help her." She rolled her head so that she now was looking at him. "That's a lot of information. Maybe I wasn't supposed to share that."

"I won't say anything. A man in love with a woman will do what he needs to do to keep her safe and happy. It's good that he supports her like he does." He reached for her hand and interlaced their fingers.

"You missed the turn to get to the highway," Catherine said as she turned her head and looked out the window.

Alex smiled. "I had one more stop in mind."

He caught the hint of a smile on her lips as he drove deeper into downtown.

A few moments later, he pulled up in front of the Brown Palace Hotel, and the valet moved around the car to Catherine's door and opened it.

Alex nodded when she'd given him a quizzical look.

He stepped out of the car, opened the back door, and pulled out two overnight bags—the one Catherine had packed, and the one he had brought with him.

"What are we doing?" Catherine smiled up at him.

"I thought this would be a nice change of pace for the night."

"You had this planned?"

Alex grinned. "I did."

"Even before I told you I loved you?"

"Reservations were made yesterday."

"Did you know I was going to tell you what I told you?"

Alex shook his head. "No, that only sweetened the pot."

The smile that formed on her lips was exactly what he'd been looking for. Everything changed tonight, he thought. Everything.

CATHERINE WALKED THROUGH THE REVOLVING DOOR AND followed Alex to the front counter. As he checked in, she stood and took in the ambiance of the lobby's atrium. It had been years since she'd been to the hotel. No doubt it had been with Rachel and their mothers for tea at Christmas, and then the lobby had transformed into something magical with its multi-story chandelier, which was hung for the holidays.

Now the lobby buzzed with people having drinks and mingling. A man played the piano, and conversations hummed in the background.

"Are you ready?" Alex asked as he picked up the bags.

Catherine nodded and walked side by side with him to the elevator. When they were inside, he pressed the button.

Alex looked down at her, and she caught his glance. "I never told you how beautiful you look tonight."

She felt the heat rise in her cheeks. "Thank you. I have a pile of clothes on my bed, which I tried on every piece before I settled on this dress."

"You made the right call."

When the doors opened, Alex walked down the open hallway, which overlooked the lobby. The noise filtered up and Catherine smiled in the moment.

Alex stopped in front of a room, set down the bags, and unlocked the door with the key card. He nodded toward Catherine to walk in as he gathered the bags.

Catherine had never been in one of the rooms. She took in the ambiance as she walked in, but then let out a little squeal of delight when she saw the bottle of champagne in a bucket of ice, two glasses, and a plate of strawberries.

She turned as the door closed behind her, and Alex set the bags on the floor.

"Are you surprised?" he asked as he moved toward her.

"Extremely," she admitted as he gathered her in his arms.

"I didn't expect you to tell me you loved me," Alex said pressing a kiss to her lips. "I expected to tell you tonight."

Catherine rested her forehead to his. "You did?"

"I did."

"Not just to have sex with me?"

She saw the flash of annoyance in his eyes, but the warmth returned. "I don't ever want you to think that."

"I don't. I'm sorry I said that."

"Catherine, I do love you. This entire thing has been one surprise after another. I'm just not sure I'm worthy of it."

Catherine lifted her fingers into his hair, closed her eyes, and breathed in the scent of his cologne. "We're both worthy of it." She opened her eyes and looked into his. "Any doubts I had about you from the past, they're cemented there—in the past. I want to be with who you are today, right now. But, Alex, I think I've always loved you, that's why not liking you stung as much as it did."

CHAPTER 23

*E*verything she said to him undid him a bit more.

Alex covered her mouth with his, taking what she'd give, and falling deeper and deeper in love with her.

Catherine's tongue danced with his, her fingers tunneled in his hair, as his hands slid over the curve of her bottom.

The past week had been torturous, and he'd put that on himself, but now, now it was right. He'd never regret telling her they'd wait until she fell in love with him. Though, having her tell him she'd always loved him confused his lust driven body, but his heart understood it.

He hadn't expected her to tell him she loved him, but he'd felt it. That was all he'd been looking for, the feeling. Every night they'd spent together, and every goodbye got harder and harder. He didn't want goodbyes anymore. He wanted to fall into bed with her every night, and wake with her every morning. Deep in his heart, he wanted to do that for the rest of his life.

Catherine's fingers moved to the buttons on his shirt, and she began to release them one by one. As she parted the fabric, and pressed her hand to his skin, Alex sucked in a breath. This was the moment he'd waited for, wished for, planned for.

Picking her up, and wrapping her legs around his waist, Alex carried Catherine to the bed and gently laid her back.

"I brought the condoms," he whispered in her ear and she laughed.

"Is it bad, I hadn't considered them yet?" she asked, pushing his shirt from his body. "My heart is hammering."

Alex pressed his hand to her chest and felt the rapid beat of her heart. "I don't want to wait anymore," he confessed and Catherine laughed.

"If you do, I might explode." She wrapped her arms around his neck and pulled him down. "Make love to me, Alex."

ALEX ROLLED TO HIS BACK AND SUCKED IN AIR AS CATHERINE DID the same next to him. It was two o'clock in the morning, and they had refueled themselves on a late night cheese platter and desserts before making love again.

The room was dark, but the light from the TV flickered on the wall. The sound had been muted. They hadn't even paid attention to what had been playing for the past few hours. They were only focused on one another.

"I feel as if we're making up for lost time," Catherine laughed as she drew in another breath. "I've lost count already as to how many times we've done it."

"We should have been doing this all along. And I don't mean for the past month," Alex gasped, pressing his hand to his chest. "I'm kicking myself for not paying more attention way back when. Imagine where we could be now." He took another breath as Catherine rolled up against him, resting her head on his shoulder, and interlacing their fingers together.

"Where could we be?"

Alex lifted Catherine's fingers to his lips, kissing the tips of each finger. "Married with kids."

He felt her fingers tense against his, but she didn't pull away. "You think if we'd have gotten together years ago, we'd be married with kids?"

Alex rolled so they were facing one another. "Yes. I've been thinking a lot about it." He brushed a strand of hair from her face. "About where we go from here."

"Alex..."

"Hear me out." He ran his thumb over her lips. "It's not like we just met and we're figuring each other out. We've known each other for years."

"But we are figuring it out. Alex, we aren't who we were before. We aren't who we were in February."

"I know." Perhaps she had a point. Hadn't they all grown quite a bit since she was in high school and he was in college—and since February?

He contemplated how he felt, especially wrapped around her in the glow of the TV's light.

Cara had devastated him—broken him. She had taken his heart and shredded it. His life had never been as dark as it had when he'd found out what she'd done to him.

The nights he'd drink until he blacked out seemed like a life-time ago, but in reality it hadn't even been a year ago. And now, here he was professing his love and asking for forever from a woman he knew would never hurt him.

"I suppose I'm getting ahead of myself. I look at where Craig and Rachel are now and think that I want that. I want that with you."

Catherine lifted her hand to rake her fingers through his hair. "I love you. And don't think that my biological clock isn't ticking, because it is, but I only plan on doing it all once—getting married and having kids. Trust me when I say I wouldn't be right here right now if I didn't think there was a chance for that. I obviously don't jump into relationships." She nipped his lips with a kiss. "I just think we need a little more time. I mean you just moved back a few months ago. I just bought my first place. You just moved into your own place."

Catherine eased back and pulled him atop her. "I think it's much too late to be talking about all of this. We're tired, fueled on sugar and lust. These conversations are for when we're fully awake and sober."

"You're right," he agreed.

"So, let's do this one more time and then get some sleep. I saw that you had reservations for breakfast. I certainly don't want to miss that."

Alex lowered his head and took her mouth. "As long as you have the energy for one more round."

"I've been saving up for years. I'm sure I have the energy."

"I love you," he said softly as she gazed up into his eyes.

"I love you too."

CHAPTER 24

Catherine had to admit, as she drove away from the glorified construction trailer where she worked, it was nice to have a job she could leave in the evenings and not carry the work home in her head or in her heart.

Even though most of her adult career had been spent on the administrative end of education, she'd taken home worries each night. And, when Rachel had been the subject of a school shooting, it had become too personal to stay.

The few items Catherine had to hunt down that day, the three meetings, and the sixty phone calls she made had her exhausted, but now the work was done until the morning. As it was Thursday, it was nacho night with Rachel, and Catherine had a lot she needed to talk to her best friend about.

When Catherine arrived at the restaurant, she walked straight into the bar area, where Rachel sat at one of the tall tables. And as usual, the plate of nachos was already on the table.

"Maybe we should reconsider our time," Catherine said as she kissed Rachel on the cheek and climbed up onto the chair. "I work further away now."

"I don't mind getting here and ordering. It occupies my head.

School is back in session, and I'm at home. I don't really know what to do with myself."

Catherine reached her hand out and covered Rachel's. "You're growing a baby, and you're still recovering. Don't sell yourself short on that."

"I know. My therapist and I talk about it every week. If I wasn't pregnant, maybe I could have gone back and dealt with it. But, I'm doing the right thing."

"You are." Catherine pulled her hand back and picked up the water that waited for her, and took a sip. "You're feeling okay?"

"I'm fine," Rachel said running her hand over her stomach which was larger than it had been when they'd gone to dinner, Catherine thought. "So what's new with you?" Rachel asked, as if she expected the gossip that was coming her way.

Catherine pulled a chip from the platter and bit down on it. "After dinner the other night, Alex took me to the Brown Palace."

Rachel's eyes grew wide. "You stayed the night?"

"We did."

"And…"

There wouldn't have been any denying what they'd done, because when Rachel paused, Catherine felt her cheeks fill with heat.

Rachel laughed. "God, it's about time. How was it?"

"You think I'm going to give you every detail?"

"Yes. That's what Thursdays are for. You're supposed to fill me in on everything."

"And what if he's doing the same thing?" Catherine asked as the waitress walked past their table, and she ordered a glass of wine.

"He probably is. And he's probably telling it to my husband, so don't worry about it. But I want to know."

"It was everything I ever dreamed it would be. And yes, I've dreamt of it."

"You're in love. You had sex. God, you're on the right path. When can I plan your bridal shower?"

Catherine shook her head and took another chip. "Let's not go there right now."

"Something hit a nerve. He doesn't want to get married?"

"Rach, we've been together a month."

"A month and a lifetime. What's going on?"

The waitress returned with Catherine's wine. She thanked her and then lifted it to her lips, taking a long drink. "He was talking as if he wanted to get married and have kids. I didn't know men thought of things like that, but he said he wanted what you and Craig have."

"Wow."

"Yeah, wow," she repeated. "I've always wanted that. But, c'mon. He's been back in Colorado for three months. Before that he lived far from here and was in a relationship. I can't assume that just because he's back here he's ready to settle down and be with me."

"And you know that's all crap, because you wouldn't have told him you love him and slept with him if you didn't think he was the one."

And that was when a best friend knew too much.

"Still, don't you think we should wait?"

"I hadn't seen Craig in ten years when I took the opportunity. Hell, I didn't think I'd get pregnant and married this quick, but I've never been happier either."

"The difference is that you and Craig had a past together. I don't have that with Alex. In fact, after the way I always treated him, I'm surprised I ever caught his eye at all."

"You were both just playing hard to get. And now you're both caught—and having sex," Rachel reminded her with a huge grin. "Don't wait too long."

"A month, Rach. We've been a couple for a month."

Rachel waved her hand in the air, and then picked up a chip.

"Yeah, yeah, yeah. Well, if you get married soon, I can still look good in a bridesmaid dress. If you wait too long, you're going to need to wait until this baby is born. I don't want to waddle down the aisle. And if it's after the baby is born, I'll need some time to get my body back."

Catherine laughed as she sipped her wine again. "As long as we have our timeline. We're good. I'm glad it's all about you—as always."

"Honey, someone has to lead the way. I'm here for you," she said with a wink. "Now, seriously. I want some juicy details, and spare nothing. Remember, we've shared every secret since we were ten. I don't expect you to hold out on me now. How is the infamous Alex Burke in bed?"

CHAPTER 25

*S*ince Ray had his kids for the night, boys' night was at his house. He'd ordered wings, and they'd all piled into his small living room to watch the baseball game.

The kids had made more than one comment about how they liked eating at their dad's house, since he let them eat in front of the TV.

Alex could appreciate that. He couldn't remember a time when his parents ever let him and Sarah eat in the living room. The thought made him chuckle as he lifted another wing to his already burning mouth, and pulled the meat from the bone with his teeth.

When Craig walked to the kitchen, Alex followed with his plate of bones, and dumped them in the trash.

"You want a beer or a glass of milk?" Craig asked as he pulled open Ray's refrigerator.

"It's a toss up," Alex said wiping his mouth with a napkin. "I think a shooter of milk, and a bottle of beer."

Craig laughed as he pulled out the milk carton and two bottles of beer.

Alex pulled a glass from the cupboard and poured the milk as Craig opened the bottles.

"How was your night at the hotel?" Craig asked as he waited for Alex to finish his milk.

"It was amazing," he said as he rinsed out the glass and set it in the sink. "Seriously, I couldn't have planned a better night."

Craig nodded slowly as he handed Alex a bottle. "So it moved in the right direction?"

"I'm not going to kiss and tell."

"You don't have to. I'm just saying, well, shit, I don't know what I'm saying. I guess, I'm wondering, where are things going?"

Alex took a pull from the bottle. "I love her, man. It feels fast and furious, but really, it's been building for years."

"It's just been inside there for years," he reminded him. "You've only been home for three months."

"So I've been reminded." Alex took another sip. "My life went to shit a year ago, and now I'm home, I'm with my pals, living in a house I convinced you to sell me," he teased. "Everything is just right."

"And now you have the girl."

"I do. And deep inside, I want that girl forever. I just don't think she's ready."

Craig took a long pull from his beer. "What's your hurry?"

"I don't know. I just feel as if it's all slipping by if I don't lock it down." Now he laughed. "I sound like a girl."

"You sound like a guy in love. Remember, I'm one of those."

"And in the past eight months, you've got the girl, married her, and now you're having a baby."

Craig nodded. "And I almost lost her, remember. Every day is a struggle for her, and a reminder to me how important every-thing is."

"Man, I didn't mean…"

"It's our reality. You love Catherine?"

"I do."

"And she loves you?"

Alex smiled. "She does."

"Then what the hell does it matter if it's been a month or ten years? And so you were a mess a year ago, you pulled yourself out of that, didn't you? You're not an unemployed drunk. You're a useful member of society with a job, a house, and a woman who loves you. Forget about the one that broke your heart."

That was exactly what Alex wanted to do—forget about Cara and the pain she'd caused him.

But that wasn't his motivation behind wanting a future with Catherine. He loved her. Forever seemed like the most logical next move.

CATHERINE UNLOADED THE DISHWASHER, WIPED DOWN THE SINK and the counter, and tied up the trash bag. The nachos she and Rachel had shared were heavy in her stomach, and so was the conversation they'd had.

Was she being unrealistic thinking that a month wasn't nearly long enough to be in a relationship before talking marriage and children?

Wondering if Alex had had the same conversations with his friends was making her nervous.

Part of the draw to dating Alex was that his friends were as important to him as Rachel was to her. Hadn't Catherine been around enough women who were petty about their boyfriends or husbands wanting to spend time with their friends? Yet, wasn't it supposed to be one of the first things a person did for self care?

Catherine cherished her Thursdays with Rachel, and she loved watching *the team* battle it out every Sunday morning. The rest of the week had now become time she spent with Alex when they weren't at work.

They had created a routine, even before the sex.

Wasn't a relationship just a glorified routine with someone you cherished?

Catherine opened the door to the garage and carried the trash bag out to the trash can.

Had she already committed to Alex, and her argument that they'd only been an actual couple a month was invalid?

She blew a strand of hair from her face.

He'd mentioned marriage and kids. He hadn't gotten down on one knee and proposed. Catherine knew she was making herself sick assuming he meant that they should hurry up and get married and move on to the next step.

Before she made it back into the house, she heard the doorbell.

Well, maybe it was time to think about moving things to the next level, such as giving Alex a key to her door so he didn't have to ring the doorbell to enter her house.

The thought humored her as she walked to the front door and pulled it open to him.

He smiled down at her in the glow of the porch light. God, he was handsome.

"I heard you might have some room for me tonight," he teased as he leaned against the door jamb.

"There might be some room here. Had I known, I would have saved the chores, and you could earn your keep."

Humor flashed in his eyes as a smile tugged at his lips. "I can pay," he said as he stepped through the door and scooped Catherine up in his arms.

It took her by surprise and she squealed as he kicked the door closed behind him.

"What do you say? Can I work off my debt?"

Catherine licked her lips and looked up into his dark, smoldering eyes.

It appeared that they weren't going to have time to discuss

their evenings with their friends, or future plans, or house keys. Alex carried her up the stairs to her bedroom, and they closed the door on the world.

CHAPTER 26

$\mathcal{W}$ith the towel wrapped around her hair, and another wrapped around her body, Catherine wiped away the fog from the bathroom mirror and took a long look at herself.

There was something there that hadn't been evident for as long as she could remember—happiness.

It radiated in her eyes and from her skin. She never would have guessed that it would have been Alex Burke that brought that back to her life.

The door opened to the bathroom, and a sleepy Alex walked in and behind her. His arms wrapped around her, and he pressed a kiss to her neck. Oh, she certainly could get used to this.

"You should have woken me. I would have scrubbed your back," he said, his voice still full of sleep.

"I have to get to work."

He groaned and it vibrated against her. "What's the key on the counter for?" he asked, and she looked down at it before she picked it up.

Holding the key between her fingers, Catherine turned to face

Alex. "It's for you. It's to my house." She pressed it to his hand. "I don't want you to have to ring the doorbell anymore."

The sleepiness in his eyes was replaced with a warmth. "You're giving me your key."

"I am."

Alex clutched it in his hand. "This is a very big deal. Thank you."

Why was that making her want to cry?

Catherine turned back to the mirror, pulling the towel from her wet hair. "It's really not."

Alex's arms came around her again. "Yes, it is. Thank you. I love you," he said before pressing another kiss to her neck.

CASUAL FRIDAY HAD MULTIPLE MEANINGS IN ALEX'S OFFICE. It also meant that the schedule was relaxed, so he took advantage of that.

When his mother answered the door, he was standing on the step with a box of donuts and a bouquet of flowers.

"Alex, this is my favorite day of the week," she said as she opened the door and kissed him on the cheek before taking the flowers.

His sister's car was in the driveway, as it was every Friday when he stopped for breakfast. Usually they talked about their week, and any plans for the weekend. But today, he had some things he needed to clear up in his head, and he couldn't think of two other women in the world that could help him set his mind straight.

"Since you never bring me flowers, I assume there's a long john in there with my name on it?" Sarah teased as she poured him a cup of coffee.

"Do I ever let you down?" he asked and then held up a finger when she took a breath. "In the donut department."

"Nice save, Ace."

Sarah set his coffee on the table and took one of the open chairs as Alex steadied the chair his mother was sitting in, before he sat down too.

He opened the donut box and they each took their favorite. If there had been a perk about coming home, this was certainly one of them, he thought.

"Remember Mrs. Jantz around the corner," he mother asked them collectively and they both nodded. "She died in her front yard last week pulling up weeds," their mother said nonchalantly. "Ya never know, do ya?"

Alex watched as his mother bit into the donut, seemingly unfazed by her own comment.

"I wanted to talk to you both about something," Alex said setting his donut down on the tiny plates his mother had set out in anticipation of the donut arrival.

Sarah shook her head. "You already knocked her up."

Alex set his jaw and narrowed his eyes on his sister, but his mother's giggle hadn't gone unnoticed.

"Lovely, Sarah," he scolded. "No."

"Let me guess again."

"Please don't," he discouraged. "She gave me a key to her place this morning."

"That's big."

"That's what I think." He tore the donut in front of him into pieces, but didn't eat any. "I told her I was thinking of marriage and kids."

His mother went on to eat her donut, but Sarah sat back in her chair and crossed her arms in front of her. "Okay, that's big too. You've never talked marriage and kids with anyone before."

"I think I freaked her out."

That caused Sarah to chuckle and lean her arms on the table. "Because I still don't think she likes you."

Alex was sure Catherine did like him, but it stung a little to think there'd been a time she didn't.

"What do I do?" He looked up at the women he admired most, and pleaded for an answer.

Sarah sat back in her chair again, silent. His mother took his hand, and drew his attention to her.

"Are you trying to overcome what happened last year?" she asked softly.

"I'm over that. I never loved Cara."

His mother nodded, and he knew how she felt about the woman, so there were no words.

"You haven't been home for very long. Are you trying to tie yourself back here?"

Alex gave that some thought. "I think I did that when I bought Craig's house. I came home for myself, and for you. I came home because it was time. Catherine wasn't part of that equation."

His mother nodded again.

"You haven't been together very long," his mother reminded him.

"But I've known Catherine most of my life. So we're picking up where we left off," he said.

Sarah shook her head. "No, when you left off, she didn't like you."

Alex bit down hard. Was that going to haunt him for the rest of his life? "She likes me now."

Sarah grinned. "I know. I've seen it. She's head over heels in love with you, though I can't imagine why."

Neither could he.

His mother redirected his attention back to her when she gathered his hand in hers. "There is no time limit on love. The start of it, or the end of it. If you're in love, it's there. It's good to let her know how you feel. If she's not ready, she's not ready, but if she loves you she'll be honest about not being ready, and you'll wait."

That was true. He would wait.

As his mother eased back in her seat, he saw the twinkle of joy in her eyes. The grin that formed on Sarah's lips told him that she was happy for him too.

He was going to propose to Catherine. For some reason, he just didn't want to wait any longer.

CHAPTER 27

For the next two weeks, Alex came and went from Catherine's house, with the use of his key. She was wrong, he thought as he let himself into the house, it was a big deal that she'd given it to him.

But it had been just the start to something bigger. They'd stayed at her house exclusively, mostly because sex was better without a roommate nearby.

His clothes had begun to hang in her closet, and his tooth-brush shared a space next to hers on the sink.

There was a menu on the refrigerator door, meals that they'd planned together, and shopped for. He was home first, so it was his turn to get dinner started.

They were in the thick of this.

Alex had taken a personal day, but he hadn't told Catherine about it. He got up and headed to his mother's house for break-fast, just as he did every Friday. Only after donuts and gossip, he and his sister had gone shopping.

Alex knew nothing about proposing and picking out rings, but Sarah had an opinion or two, and including her in his secret had fueled a bond between them that had long ago been forged in childhood secrets of the past.

The ring weighed heavy in his pocket. He wasn't sure when he was going to propose, but he was going to.

Thoughts zipped through his head. Should he take her to a fancy dinner? Maybe they should go on vacation. He should go to her parents and ask their blessing. Or was there an age limit on that?

Their friends should be involved. Maybe he should ask Rachel to help him plan.

He heard the garage door go up, so he walked toward the door that opened to the garage, and opened it. There was a comfort to watching her pull her car in. The very need to stand there every day for the rest of his life and watch her go through the mundane routine of collecting her things after work, and climbing out of her car appealed to him.

Were men supposed to have feelings this strong? Suddenly there was a need to know if she had a secret book of wedding plans somewhere. Had she and Rachel planned out every aspect of her dream wedding? Did she have names for kids she didn't have yet?

"Why are you standing there looking so perplexed?" Catherine asked as she climbed from her car, carrying the bag she took to work with her, and her lunch box.

Alex blinked. He probably looked a bit frazzled, now that he thought of all the things running through his head.

"I was just thinking about how nice it was to watch you pull in to the garage. It sounds silly really," he began as she walked up the steps and pressed a kiss to his lips.

"It's not silly. Last week I cried looking at your toothbrush next to mine. I wasn't sad. It said a lot. It said you were there with me. It was intimate. Does that make sense."

"More than you can imagine." Alex stepped back and let her pass.

He watched as she continued her routine by hanging her bag on the hook, and taking out the mail she'd picked up as she'd driven into the community. Next she took her lunch box to the sink and unloaded any containers that needed to be washed.

"Will you marry me?" The words had come from him without his permission. God, what had he just done?

Catherine stopped what she was doing and turned slowly to look at him.

"What?"

"Wow, I've spent all day trying to figure out how to do that romantically, and that's what I chose?" he questioned himself aloud. "You can just forget I said anything, and we..."

"Oh, I can't forget that. You've been thinking about asking me that all day?"

Well, shit!

This was it, he thought. He'd made his unconscious decision when he'd opened his mouth and let the words fall out.

Alex moved toward her, though his legs felt as if they were made of steel.

As he approached her, he put his hand in his pocket, and pulled out the small velvet pouch which held the ring he and his sister had picked out that morning.

When he looked up at Catherine, her face had gone ghost white. This wasn't going to end well, he thought. God, he should have kept his mouth shut.

He was in it now. Pulling the diamond from the pouch, he held it between his fingers.

"My sister helped me pick this out. She said you deserved something with as much brilliance as you. A cut that matched, hence the princess cut. And something that got the attention of everyone, and said that someone loved you enough to put a ring on it."

That made Catherine chuckle, but when she did, he'd noticed the tears that streamed from her eyes.

"I'd thought about planning a romantic dinner, or a vacation. Then I thought I should go ask your parents, but…"

"Damnit! Put the ring on me! Yes! I'll marry you," she croaked out the words between sobs.

Alex slid the beautiful ring on her finger, admiring it on her delicate hand. Then he lifted her chin with his finger and looked into her crystal blue eyes, which were filled with tears.

"I promise to make you happy. I know this is all so sudden, but I cannot imagine another moment without you."

Catherine lifted her arms around his neck. "I can't imagine being happier than I am right at this moment."

"You'll be happier. I promise."

She laughed as she pressed her forehead to his. "I love you so much. And, for the record, the surprise of your proposal made it so much better than if you'd planned it out, down to the minute."

"I'm glad you appreciate it. It surprised even me."

Catherine kissed him again. "We have to tell everyone."

"Okay, where do we start?"

Taking his hand, Catherine led him from the kitchen to the stairs. "We need to cement this deal first."

CHAPTER 28

"Oh-My-God!" Rachel pulled Catherine's hand toward her, nearly knocking Catherine off her feet. "Oh-My-God!" she repeated.

"I'd like to keep my hand," Catherine joked as she looked back at Alex who laughed at Rachel's antics.

Rachel lifted her eyes from the ring to Alex. "You didn't say anything."

"I suppose that depends on who you ask. I talked to your husband about it."

Craig held up his hands in surrender. "For the record, he didn't tell me he was going to propose. He only told me how he feels."

Rachel tugged on Catherine's hand again. "I'm so happy for you," she squealed and pulled her in for a hug. "So when is this going to happen? Remember I have a timeline."

Catherine laughed as she eased back from Rachel's grasp and looked down at her hand to admire the ring. "I'm very familiar with your timeline. We haven't made any plans yet. In fact, you're the first people we told."

Alex wrapped his arm around Catherine's waist. "My sister

helped me buy the ring, but I hadn't anticipated proposing the way I did. I guess I couldn't hold it in any longer," he said, then pressed a kiss to the top of Catherine's head.

Rachel rested her hands on the swell of her belly. "We need an engagement party."

"We do?" Catherine laughed at the thought.

"Oh, yes we do. We can plan it and have it at Alex's house." She shifted a glance in his direction. "You have the best yard. And, if we have it in the next few weeks, it'll still be nice enough to have it in the yard."

Alex nodded. "Okay, let's have a party. But before you send out the invites or tell anyone, we're going to head to my mother's house and her parents' house and let them in on our little secret."

Rachel blew out a breath. "Hurry and do that, then call me. I promise not to say a word, but I'm so excited for you, that might only last a few hours."

Catherine pulled Rachel in and hugged her. The spontaneity of their engagement was one thing, but Rachel's reaction had made it that much sweeter.

ALEX'S MOTHER HAD BEEN GRACIOUS, AND THOUGH SHE'D KNOWN of his plans, her excitement for their wedding made Catherine happy.

As they'd sat at her dining room table over dinner, his mother had pulled out her wedding album and shared her love story with Catherine. Of course it had been a story that Alex and Sarah were more than familiar with, so they too chimed in, mocking their mother all in good fun.

. . .

WHEN THEY'D SAT DOWN WITH HER PARENTS, CATHERINE WAS A little disappointed that they hadn't had the same excitement that Rachel or Alex's mother had.

"You're not planning a holiday wedding, are you?" her mother had asked still holding Catherine's hand, examining the ring.

"We haven't talked about a date yet," Catherine admitted. "Rachel's baby is due in January, so we will probably wait."

With cool eyes, her mother looked up at her. "It's not Rachel's wedding. I don't see where it should matter if she's having a baby or not."

The words stung, but Catherine knew her mother didn't mean them as they were directed. What she knew was they had reservations about Alex, and who would blame them? They had reservations about the entire team of boys that hung around Rachel's house back then.

"I'm very happy, mama. I hope you're happy for me," she added and her mother's eyes softened.

"Of course I am. This is wonderful news," her mother's voice had the motherly tone she'd expected in the first place, and her arms comforted Catherine as she pulled her in and hugged her.

ALEX TAPPED HIS FINGERS ON THE STEERING WHEEL AS HE maneuvered the highway on a crowded Saturday afternoon. His mind was stirred up, and it was starting to affect his mood.

Catherine's parents should have been just a bit more gracious, he thought. She deserved the same excitement from them as she'd received from her best friend and his own mother.

It wasn't as if she'd announced her engagement to someone they'd never met, or as if they didn't know she was in a relation-ship with Alex.

Catherine touched his thigh, and he flinched.

"Sorry," he said, taking her hand.

"You seem preoccupied."

"I guess I am." He lifted her hand to his lips and kissed her fingers as he drove toward home. "Sorry."

"You keep saying that. What's bothering you?"

Alex shook his head, keeping his eyes on the road. "Nothing."

"You're upset that my parents didn't make a bigger deal about this, aren't you?"

Now he turned and looked at her. Luckily his eyes were covered behind his sunglasses. He turned back to watch the road. "Okay, it caught me off guard. I thought we'd get the same reaction as we had from everyone else. I guess I should have asked their blessing. I just…"

"It's not that," Catherine said, her voice dipping lower.

"What was it?"

Alex knew it was bad when she pulled her hand back from his and shifted her attention out the window. "They're worried for me."

"Because I'm some player, right?"

"Alex…"

"Isn't that what you told me? Isn't that your issue with me?"

He shifted another look her way, only this time there wasn't sadness or concern on her face, it was lit with anger.

"Have you looked at my freaking finger lately? Do you think I have an issue with you?"

"You did though," he argued as he took the exit off the highway. "Let's think back to when I started coming back around. You said that to me."

"I did. But I think I told you that I noticed all of that because I was noticing you."

He didn't like the way it felt either way. "I'm not going to leave and, hell, I don't know, cheat on you or change my mind. I'm not really sure what my twenty-year-old self is supposed to have done that now affects my thirty-plus-year-old self."

Catherine gripped her hands in her lap. "They knew how I felt about you back then. They didn't like me hanging around Rachel's when all the college guys were around."

"Then why did you?" He didn't like the tone of his voice.

"Because it was exciting. But at the same time, I was super protective of Rachel, and I didn't want her to get hurt."

"What about you? It seems your parents were worried. You weren't?"

"I didn't think anyone noticed me."

And hadn't they covered that topic already? He'd noticed.

Alex made his next turn and gripped the steering wheel again. "Your parents are leery of me. Why?"

He shifted a glance toward her to see her chewing her bottom lip.

"Because it didn't matter how many of those guys went from girl to girl, party to party, my only problem was when you did it."

"It shouldn't have been any of your business."

"Right," he heard the tears in her voice. "But I made it my business. I'd get all worked up over it and take it home with me as if you did it to me."

Alex nodded. "You set the impression."

"And then you came for Rachel after Craig disappeared."

"What a bastard, huh?"

"Alex…"

He shook his head. He was going to need some time to process his past and how it affected his future.

Alex took her hand and gave it a squeeze. "I'm going to need some time with this."

CHAPTER 29

The entire conversation had twisted him up. Alex didn't like Catherine's parents' reaction, and he didn't like the explanation she gave for their reactions either.

The worst part was facing it.

Alex pulled into his own driveway, after having taken Catherine home and leaving again.

They'd been together nonstop lately, maybe they needed a little break. One night apart, and he could wrap his head around what had happened.

When he'd left Catherine crying, he assured her he'd be back in the morning. There was no reason to assume otherwise.

Alex walked into the house, through the back door as he always did, dropping his keys on the counter, and pulling open the refrigerator. He took out a beer, studied it, and then put it back.

In the mood he was in, it would be easy to drink himself out of it. But tonight, he needed to feel the pain and the guilt associated with it.

"Christ! You scared the hell out of me," Bruce stood in the doorway with a golf club in his hand.

"I just came home. What's the problem?" Alex snapped, took a bottle of water out of the refrigerator, and twisted off the top.

"Oh, I don't know. You haven't been here at all in a week and hardly a handful of times in the past month." Bruce lowered the club, moved to the refrigerator, and took out a beer. "You could give a guy some notice."

"Hey, asshat, I'm home," Alex said as Bruce shut the door to the refrigerator and twisted the top off the bottle.

"You're in a mood. God, did she come to her senses and kick your ass out?"

"That would seem right, wouldn't it? Alex Burke finds the perfect woman, proposes, and gets kicked to the curb. Right up my alley."

Bruce lowered the bottle before he sipped. "You proposed to her?"

"Word didn't get back to you yet?"

"No. Am I the last to know?"

"I have no idea," Alex grunted the words and walked past Bruce toward the living room.

He looked around the room, which hadn't been touched in a month, and fell into his favorite recliner. And in true from of a good friend, Bruce followed, sitting on the couch with his beer in his hand.

"What's going on?" Bruce asked, his voice steady and calm as if he were a therapist.

Alex shook his head. "Ya know when you're a young man, not too bad looking, smooth with the ladies?"

"No. That wasn't me."

Alex laughed. That was true. "Well, let me tell you, it bites you in the fricking ass years later."

"Someone came after you?"

"No. My reputation seems to have preceded me when it comes to Catherine and her family."

"Someone you were with?"

127

Alex chuckled. "All of them really. It appears that my fiancée had a thing for me back when."

"You had eyes on her too, if I remember correctly."

"And that would have been inappropriate, for the most part," Alex reminded him. "But yeah. Anyway, when she'd see me go off with someone, I guess she went home and verbally bashed me. Or some shit like that. I don't actually know. Let's just say after years of not hearing the good, and then I just show back up, they have their reservations."

"Got it."

"I'm not who I was when I was in college."

"None of us are."

"And that's a damn good thing."

Bruce lifted his beer in salute. "Amen."

"I just thought they should have been a little more gracious. Rachel," he laughed, "well, Rach was more excited than we were. Okay, almost more."

"Rachel knows who you really are. She's always had your back. Always," he emphasized again.

Rachel had always understood him, and that would bode well for him when it came to Catherine.

Catherine. Wasn't that all that mattered?

Alex rested his head back against the chair.

Catherine loved him. She believed in him. There were no secrets. He'd never done anything wrong, well no more than break a few hearts, but in the end he'd been the one left alone.

It wasn't as if her parents had forbade them from getting married. So, they didn't jump up and down gleefully. Hell, they'd shaken his hand when he walked out of their house.

"So what are you going to do? Head back?" Bruce asked.

"No. We need a night to just calm down."

"Shitty way to start off an engagement."

Alex nodded. "I think I need to go back to her parents' house and talk to them. Catherine deserves that."

"You deserve that. You're a great guy. Anyone would be lucky to have you as an in-law."

"Thanks."

Bruce nodded as he stood. "Just for the record. I'm a great guy too."

"No doubt."

"You'd be lucky to have me as an in-law."

Alex growled. "My sister is off limits."

That sent Bruce into a bout of laughter. "It never gets old, dude. Never. But on a serious note, what are you guys going to do about your living arrangement? Do I need to find a place? Are you going to rent out this one? If so, can I get the upstairs?"

Alex let out a long breath. "I have no idea."

"No pressure. Just let me know. But, seriously, if you come home, just let me know. I'm getting used to you being gone. I don't want to crack open your skull with a nine-iron."

"I'd appreciate it," Alex laughed as Bruce walked out of the room leaving him with just his thoughts.

He sipped his water. He was going to change and get cleaned up, then head back to the Anderson's house. They needed to know his intentions, and they needed to give him their blessing. It was that important.

Alex drank down his water and stood. The photo of him and Sarah at his college graduation caught his eye on the bookshelf. He chuckled to himself. Yeah, Bruce would be great in-law material, but it would be over Alex's dead body that he would be his.

CHAPTER 30

*B*efore she had ever gone to bed, Catherine had received the text. *Meet me at the Y in the morning for basketball. I'll catch a ride with Bruce and go home with you. Lots to tell you. I love you. Good night.*

She'd reread the text at least thirty times.

For some reason she wanted to read anger into it, but it was worded with *I love you,* and *lots to tell you* as if something good had happened after he'd left her. That couldn't be it, he'd been upset, but as she'd recalled, he hadn't been angry.

Sitting in the parking lot of the YMCA, Catherine tried to collect her emotions. She twisted the sparkling diamond ring on her finger. This was a hiccup in their relationship, that was all. In time they'd have another. Perhaps one of them would sleep on the couch then or spend the night at a friend's. That was what couples did when they argued, right?

How the hell was she really supposed to know? The last relationship she'd been in was over four years ago, and though it had lasted equally as long, they'd been young. There hadn't been family involvement, or a group of friends. In fact, they'd both been so young there weren't even pasts to contend with.

Everything with Alex was new—even if it was built on a friendship that was old.

She blew out a breath, closed her eyes tight, and willed the anxiety to cease. When she opened her eyes, she saw him.

Alex was walking toward her car, and he was smiling. What could he possibly have to smile about?

Taking one more deep breath, Catherine opened the door, and stepped out of her car.

By the time she was out of the car, Alex was to her. His hands came to her cheeks, and without a word, he lowered his mouth to hers and kissed her as if nothing had ever been wrong between them.

"I love you," he said softly. "I love you."

Catherine batted back tears that stung her eyes. "You're not angry with me?"

Alex kissed her again. "I never was. I just needed to sort through things. I've done that."

"We're okay?"

He brushed his thumb over her cheek. "Better than okay. I went back to your parents' house last night and talked to them. I asked them for their blessing, and apologized for proposing without it. We cleared up some feelings, and your mother hugged me before I left."

Catherine's lip trembled as she looked up at him. "You went to my parents' house?"

"I had to."

"You didn't have to, but you did."

"I'm not that guy they believed me to be. And I'm ashamed that I might have been. That's in the past. I'm devoted to you. I swear."

Catherine lifted her arms around his neck and his hands moved to her waist. "I love you. I'm so sorry all of this happened."

"It won't be the last time."

That caused her to laugh. "I was thinking that while I was sitting here. We'll go through this again."

"Of course we will. I'm sure inside you still have some doubts about me. You can't make all the hard feelings go away in a few months."

"There are no doubts."

Alex let out a hum. "We'll see." He kissed her forehead. "New business. Bruce wants to know where he's supposed to live," he said grinning down at her.

"We haven't even discussed that."

"I think more than anything, he just doesn't want me dropping in like I did last night. He came after me with a nine-iron."

Catherine pressed her hands to his chest. "Did he hit you?"

Alex laughed and shook his head. "He was prepared. That's all."

"Good," she sighed. "There's so much to think about. Where will we live? We need to set a date. Rachel wants to have that engagement party."

Alex leaned in and kissed her again. "We're not in any hurry. We're committed to each other. That is the most important thing. Married or not, I'm yours and you're mine."

"Forever, Alex."

"I promise. Nothing can come between us—nothing."

WHILE *THE TEAM*, AND THE SISTER, GRUNTED AND CHIRPED AT ONE another about their lack of skill, Rachel and Catherine sat on the bleachers and planned an engagement party.

"We're already into October in two weeks," Rachel said as she studied the calendar on her phone. "But that's okay. I still think if you do it at Alex's house, you'll have room. No offense, you don't have enough parking at your house."

"Well, when I bought it, I was sure you'd be the only one to ever visit. Who knew this was how our year was going to turn out?"

Rachel laughed and ran her hand over her belly. "Who indeed."

"He asked my parents for their blessing last night," Catherine said in a hushed tone, though no one would have ever heard her anyway.

"Wow. How did your mom take it when you told her you were engaged to Alex Burke?"

"She should have taken it better than she did. It's not like she didn't know I was seeing him."

"Dating and marriage are two different things."

"I suppose. But he took the initiative to go and talk to them."

"He's a good man."

"So you keep saying."

"And I mean it." Rachel adjusted her position on the bleacher. "Maybe you should hurry and get pregnant."

"What?" Catherine laughed and nearly choked on it. "Talk about ramping things up."

Rachel smiled, rubbing her hand over her belly. "Think about it. Our babies could grow up together."

Catherine looked out over the court where the friends playing ball called one another names, and Sarah took the ball and laid it up to increase the score.

"I'm sure he won't want to wait. I don't think I'm the one with my biological clock ticking," Catherine humored, but the thought was now planted. Rachel was right. Her baby could grow up with Rachel's baby. Was that what Alex wanted too? Their children to grow up with the children of his friends?

The thought was appealing.

But first things first. She needed to get him home and they needed to settle all of the feelings that were hurt the night before. What better way to move on than with makeup sex?

CHAPTER 31

*A*lex sat on his own bed, in his own house, and watched Catherine add the small diamonds he'd given her for their engagement to her ears.

"God, you're beautiful," he said as she lowered her hands and spun around in the tight red dress she wore. Her blonde curls bounced at her shoulders, and her blue eyes sparkled.

"Thank you for the earrings. I think the ring is supposed to have been the engagement present."

Alex held out his hand and she took it in hers. He pulled her to him, wrapping his arms around her waist. "You deserve all the pretty things," he said tucking a piece of her hair behind her ear and touching the shimmering diamond. "I can't wait to marry you."

"Thank you for waiting until Rachel's baby is born."

"She did always run the show," he teased. "Maybe you'll get some baby fever when her baby gets here."

Catherine's eyes opened wide when he mentioned it. "Now you really do sound like Rachel."

Alex chuckled. "How's that?"

"She thinks we should get on it and have a baby. Then our kids can grow up together and be instant best friends."

The smile that tugged at his cheeks probably made him look like an idiot, but he couldn't help it. "I like that idea."

"I was afraid you would. That's why I didn't mention it."

"You don't want kids?"

He was sure the color had drained from her face. "It's not that I don't want kids. I just think there is a process. First we get married. Then we get settled. Then we talk about it. Then we plan it…"

"And then all the fun is sucked out of it."

And that had obviously offended her.

Catherine moved to turn away, but Alex caught her and pulled her back to him. "We'll plan it. I'm sorry."

"Don't be sorry. It's old-fashioned of me. But I can't let it go."

"Do you hold it against Rachel for being pregnant before she got married?"

"No. This seems to just be in my own case. I don't know how to shake it from my head."

"But what if it happens? We're still talking six months before we get married. I'm not keeping my hands off of you." He thought better about that. "I don't want to keep my hands off you. I rather enjoy what we have going on."

Catherine leaned her head against his. "We'd deal with it."

And wasn't that the least romantic thing she could have said?

Alex decided the discussion had put a damper on the party that Rachel had planned, and he didn't want to ruin it. Pressing a kiss to Catherine's lips, he soaked in the blue of her eyes.

"I love you. I'm so happy that we're going to get married. I can't think of anything better than a long, happy life with you."

Now she smiled, and that put him at ease. "I have a present for you too. Not a physical one. Well, not really."

Alex eased back. "I'm intrigued."

"We've talked about it very briefly, but I think we should move back here and live in your house."

Now he felt the smile on his mouth widen. "Really?"

Catherine nodded. "We'll rent my place to Bruce, if he wants. It might be out of his way. But we both work in Denver, and this is much closer. It has a yard, and the neighbors aren't so close they can look into our house." She chuckled. "The garage fits two cars and…"

"I'm sold. You don't have to tell me any more. You have no idea how much that means to me."

"We'll discuss it with Bruce. And he has plenty of time to decide."

Alex stood, cupped Catherine's face in his hands, and lowered his mouth to hers. This was the start of a perfect life, and he couldn't imagine what he'd ever done right to deserve it.

RACHEL HAD TAKEN CONTROL OF PLANNING THE PARTY, AND Catherine wasn't disappointed. She understood her friend needed something to occupy her mind. It was a healing of sorts. And anything Catherine could do to help Rachel heal, she was going to do it. In this case, she happened to get an amazing party as well.

The weather held out, and the back yard was filled with more people than Catherine could have imagined. There were people who had worked with her and Rachel from the school district, and new colleagues from Ray's construction business. Childhood friends, and cousins from both sides of her family.

There was no skimping on guests that came to honor Alex either, which included family, friends, and others who had played basketball with *the team* over the years.

Catherine wondered just how much healing that brought to

Rachel as well. Was it moving past something, or embracing it? She wasn't sure.

"I'd like to make a toast," she heard Alex's voice rise over the crowd.

Catherine turned to see him standing on the back step, and she walked toward him. He reached out his hand and she took it. When she was next to him, he wrapped an arm around her waist, and pressed a kiss to her lips.

"For those of you who had your doubts, Alex Burke can be tamed," he said and everyone laughed. "But, this beautiful woman, right here, has always had a part of my heart—always. I just want to honor her for a moment, and in front of everyone, I want to tell her how much I love her." He looked down into her eyes, and now it was if he were talking to only her. "I will never run from any problems that arise. I will never leave you to fight for anything without me. I will be your partner in all things good and bad. Catherine, you are my everything. Without you, I'm nothing. You make me want to be a better person. You make me want to be a perfect husband, and someday a father. I can't imagine my life without you in it, and I never want to."

Catherine lifted her hand to his cheek. "You'll never have to."

She pressed her lips to his, and he gathered her in as everyone applauded, and a few of their friends hollered things like *about time*, and *who would have thought*. But Catherine knew that her perfect life was with Alex.

As she eased back, she noticed Alex's eyes shift, and the attention of the crowd around them was focused on two police officers who had walked up the driveway.

Bruce was the first to move to them. "Officers, how can we help you?"

"We're looking for Alex Burke."

Catherine watched as Alex's face drained of color. He looked out over the crowd as if to place his mother and sister there.

When he found them, he took Catherine's hand and walked toward the officers.

"I'm Alex Burke."

The female officer scanned a look over him. "Can we have a word with you out front?"

"Of course," he said as he opened the gate and walked toward the driveway, Catherine's hand still in his.

"You might want to come alone," the officer said.

"This is Catherine Anderson. She's my fiancée. I'd be more comfortable if she were with me."

The officer nodded and followed them to the front yard.

Once they were away from the others, Alex turned toward them. "How can I help you?"

The officer shifted a look between Alex and Catherine, and Catherine gripped Alex's hand tighter.

"We're here on behalf of the Baltimore police department."

"Baltimore?"

"They're looking for you."

"I've never been to Baltimore."

The officer bit down on her lip. "Are you sure you wouldn't like to chat alone?"

"I'm not guilty of anything. I'm fine talking with her here," he said, as he looked down at Catherine.

"Cara Tobin," the officer said, and Catherine heard the sharp inhale Alex took.

"Yes?"

"You know her?"

He exchanged a glance with Catherine again. "I do. We were involved a year ago. Or we became uninvolved about a year ago, is more like it."

The officer nodded again. "Well, she was killed in a car accident two days ago."

Catherine gripped his hand even tighter as he lifted his other hand to cover his mouth. "That's horrible." He took a moment. "I don't mean to sound rude, but what does that have to do with me?"

The officer narrowed her eyes on him. "Your daughter was with her. She's safe, but..."

Alex stumbled back, pulling his hand from Catherine's and gripping his chest. "My what?"

"Your daughter."

"I don't have a daughter."

"According to her birth certificate you do."

CHAPTER 32

*A*lex had heard the words. The officer had said them right to his face, but his brain had clouded. No, that's not what she had said. There was absolutely no way that he had a child and didn't know about it.

From the corner of his eye, he saw Catherine sway. Moving to her, he grabbed her arms and eased her to the ground before she fell.

Kneeling next to her, he cupped her cheek with his hand. Her face had gone ghost white, and her eyes rolled back before she sucked in a breath and he knew she was okay.

"I'll get you some water," he said and Catherine shook her head.

"I'm fine. I'm fine!" she shouted, though he wasn't sure she knew that's what she was doing. Her eyes were still wide, and he saw the tears beginning to well in them. "You have a baby?"

Alex shook his head. "No." He looked up at the police officer, still kneeling next to Catherine. "I haven't talked to Cara Tobin since January."

The officer shrugged. "I'm delivering news," she said. "I have the information for you to contact Baltimore."

"There's no need for me to contact them. I don't have a kid."

"Well, there is a baby in foster care. Your name is on the birth certificate, and for the sake of that baby, we need you to contact them."

Alex rose to his feet. "Let me get her situated, and I'll get the information from you."

The officer nodded.

Alex helped Catherine to her feet. Instead of going around the house, he walked her to the front door and pulled it open. As they stepped inside, he led her to the couch.

"Sit. I'm going to get you some water and find Rachel," he said.

"You have a baby."

"I don't have a baby. There's some mistake."

"You have a baby with another woman," she sobbed.

Alex knelt down in front of her. "She might have put my name on the birth certificate, but remember why I'm not with her. There are plenty of men who could be that baby's father. Sit here. I'll be right back."

He stood and walked to the kitchen. Opening the refrigerator, he pulled out a bottle of water, walked to the back door, and scanned the yard for Rachel.

As if she'd known he was looking for her, she walked across the yard to him. "What's going on?"

"I need you."

Rachel stepped inside the house. "You're scaring me. What do the police want? Where's Catherine?"

"She's on the couch. There's some news that has her upset. I'm sure she'll fill you in. I need to go back out and talk to them."

Rachel reached her hand out to his arm. "Are you in some kind of trouble?"

Alex swallowed hard. He wasn't so sure. "No. She'll fill you in."

He handed Rachel the water and she followed him back to the living room.

Alex knelt in front of Catherine. "I'm going to go talk to them. Sit with Rachel. I'll be right back."

He walked out of the house and back to the officer who waited for him.

The woman who had told him about the baby handed him a piece of paper. "Here's the information."

"I just need to call them and clear this up?"

"Sir, I understand that you might not know about this baby. But there is a reason she put your name on that birth certificate. There is a five month old baby in the system and she needs a home."

"I feel for her. I really do, but I'm not her father."

The officer nodded. "Call them. I'm sure they can walk you through the process."

Alex stood there, the piece of paper in his hand. He was numb as he watched the officers pull away from the house. What had Cara done to him?

He knew deep down in his soul that baby wasn't his. Why had she put his name on that damn certificate?

And Catherine—how was he going to mend this with her? She'd forever have doubt in her mind.

Alex folded the paper and tucked it into his pocket as he walked up the front step and into the house. Catherine sat in Rachel's arms, sobbing. This wasn't how he'd imagined them starting their life together.

Rachel looked up at him. "Are you kidding me?"

"Don't accuse. There is so much going on here, just don't accuse me."

"I'm not accusing. But, God!"

He nodded. "I know. Let us have a moment. Just let everyone know we're okay."

Rachel nodded and gave Catherine a kiss on top of her head as she stood and walked out of the room.

Alex sat down on the couch and gathered Catherine's hands

in his. "I love you," he said, but she avoided looking up at him. "I said…"

"I heard you," she snapped. "I can't stop crying."

"Honey, I'm going to sort this out."

When she lifted her eyes to meet his, they were red and her lip trembled. "Sort it out. There's a baby out there being tossed around with your name attached to her."

"And Cara did that. I didn't know anything about it."

"It lines up," she said as she wiped her eyes. "She could be your baby."

The heat under his collar was intensifying. "You don't know how vindictive she could be."

"All the more reason for her to have a baby and not tell you."

Her words socked him in the gut. "Listen, let's pull it together and get back to our party."

"Are you kidding? Why bother?"

Alex gathered her hands in his. "Don't do this. Don't let something that someone said ruin what we have."

"What do we have? Something built on a lie?"

"Not my lie." He lifted her hands to his lips. "I swore to you, in front of all those people, that I'd never run. And I said I'd be with you through good and bad. Well, it appears this is bad."

"What if she's yours?"

He didn't want to think about it. In his head, it didn't add up. "I'm not even going to think about that. Tomorrow I'll call Baltimore. They'll let me know what I need to do to clear this up."

"What if…"

"Catherine, no what ifs. You are my everything, remember? This is just a misunderstanding. Nothing changes. I love you. I'm going to marry you."

"I'm scared."

So was he.

CHAPTER 33

*A*lex held Catherine all night long, though he wasn't sure if it was to comfort her or him. She hadn't said much, but neither had he. His mind raced, and sleep hadn't come.

They'd chosen to not go to the YMCA for Sunday basketball. Catherine didn't want to see anyone, and Alex just wasn't sure what he was supposed to tell everyone, though by now, everyone at that party had to have known what happened.

He'd left the house under the guise that he was going to get them some breakfast, but as he sat in the parking lot at the grocery store, he held the piece of paper in his hand that the officer had given him, and it shook. The phone call he'd just made had rocked him to the core.

Cara Tobin had been run off the road by a drunk driver and killed instantly. Her daughter, whom they wouldn't tell him her name or her exact location, had been recovered from the scene with only minor scrapes.

The baby, who was five months old, was in the state's care in the foster system. Cara's only living relative was her father, and he didn't want anything to do with a baby.

Alex had counted back nine months from May multiple times, and each time it made him sick.

Cara had left him for good in October, when he'd found out that she'd been cheating on him. That was when he'd spiraled out of control. He was solidly drunk from October through January. He sobered up the night she'd called him six times in a row, but he'd never answered. When she left voice messages, he'd erased them without listening to them. He'd wanted nothing to do with her.

Sickness washed over him. No matter who fathered her child, she'd been pregnant while they were still together and she hadn't said a word.

Alex scrubbed his hands over his face. This was a nightmare— an absolute nightmare.

He looked at the clock on his radio screen. It had been an hour since he'd left the house. Catherine would be growing more anxious with him gone.

Before he put the car in drive, Alex took one last long breath. Never in his life had he felt as low as he did in that moment, and that included the months when he was black out drunk.

Nine months before the baby's birth had been August. August had been when he and Cara had gone on vacation and spent the entire weekend in a hotel room.

~

CATHERINE HAD LEFT HIM A NOTE. IT WAS COWARDLY, BUT SHE needed some space.

Rachel had stayed home from the basketball game too, so Catherine headed straight for her house. At the moment she was the only person Catherine could talk to, but she was damn sure Rachel would always side with Alex.

There were cinnamon rolls on a plate, a kettle of hot water on the stove, and a collection of teas on the table waiting to be chosen.

Catherine sat down at the table and waited for Rachel to carry over the kettle and join her.

The moment she sat down across from her, Catherine began to cry.

Rachel reached for her hands and held them. "Let it out," she said. "Just let it all out."

"What if it's true? What if he has a baby?"

"Then he has a lot of responsibility coming his way."

Catherine pulled back one of her hands and wiped away the tears. "This isn't a joke."

"No, it's not. There's a little girl out there who lost her mother and doesn't have her father around. Now, if that father is Alex, then he'll do what's right. If it's not Alex, he'll still do what's expected of him."

"Meaning?"

"Meaning he will call. He'll get the information. He'll take a test or something."

Catherine sucked in a breath. She was right. Rachel would defend him.

"What if that test comes back as a match?"

Rachel shrugged. "I don't know, sweetheart. I just don't know."

The tears were back, and Rachel pulled Catherine into her arms and held her as she cried.

Catherine couldn't help but feel selfish sitting there crying in Rachel's arms. The man she loved was facing his own crisis, and all she could think about was what that meant to her. What opportunities it had stolen from her. God, she was pathetic.

She'd gone into that relationship knowing Alex had been in another relationship less than a year ago. Why was it so easy to accept that his heart had been broken enough that he'd fallen into a black hole of despair and climbed back out, but she couldn't wrap her head around the fact that he might have actually cared for the woman he was in the relationship with.

Everything had been about Catherine from the moment the officer said Alex had a daughter. It had been her feelings about him that had nearly ruined everything before it even started. It had been her virtue he was protecting when she'd confided that she'd only been with one other man. Hell, it was because of her best friend that they were waiting to get married so she fit in a damn dress.

But she just wasn't sure she could handle it if he fathered a child.

Sitting back, she pressed her hand to her stomach. The very thought of it made her sick.

"Eat something," Rachel said, pushing the plate of cinnamon rolls toward her. "Just sit here as long as you need to. I can call Craig and have him stay out for a while."

That too was selfish, but Catherine nodded. She just needed a little more time to wallow in her selfish misery.

Rachel nodded. "Let me call him."

She stood from the table leaving Catherine alone with her thoughts.

How was she going to pull herself out of this? Alex needed her support. What would give her the strength to stand by his side while he went through this?

And what was going to keep her from running if indeed that baby was his?

CHAPTER 34

*A*lex held Catherine's note in his hand.

I'll be at Rachel's. I need some time. C.

There were no *I love yous*, no promises of return times, and nothing that said, *I'm sorry you're going through this.* Alex was absolutely alone to wallow in his misery and what ifs.

He picked up the bag of food he'd ordered and threw it into the trash can. He wasn't hungry.

A year ago, Cara had crushed him. What she'd done was harsh, and cold. Six men. Six!

It wasn't as if she'd gotten involved with someone at work and they had a relationship. No, Alex meant so little that she bounced from bed to bed, and then came home to him.

The thought disgusted him. He'd been truthful and faithful. Now he was happy, and had found true love, and because of Cara Tobin, he was on the verge of losing that too.

But, the realization was, if the baby was his, he'd bring her home. No one deserved to lose their mother and never know their father. And if she was his daughter, he didn't want anyone else raising her.

However, if he brought her home, he'd lose Catherine forever.

Alex paced the floor in the kitchen, then, he walked out of the house, locking the door behind him, and went back home.

BRUCE WAS IN THE BACK YARD WHEN ALEX PULLED UP. HE WAS cleaning up the party, which Alex and Catherine had abruptly left.

He lifted his head as Alex walked through the gate. "Hey, man. You doing okay?"

Alex shook his head. "I'm numb."

Bruce dropped the bag in his hand and moved to Alex, enveloping him a hug that caused Alex to instantly sob.

Just as a brother would, Bruce kept his arms around him.

When they parted, Bruce's hands rested on Alex's shoulders. "Let's get some coffee. We can talk it out. We can sit in silence. We can go shoot some pool," he offered. "But I think it'd do you some good to talk it out."

Alex nodded and headed toward the back door.

By the time Bruce walked into the house, Alex had the coffee brewing. The lack of sleep was settling into his body, and the amount of information he'd received that morning buzzed in his head.

Bruce walked to the sink and washed his hands, then leaned up against the counter as he dried his hands.

"Do you think she's your baby?" he asked.

"Everyone knows?"

Bruce shrugged. "Your mom was pretty upset. I talked to Sarah late last night."

He hadn't even thought about the effect this would have on his mother.

"I go in tomorrow to take a paternity test. I should know in two days." He scrubbed his hands over his face. "Timelines add up," he admitted. "She would have been pregnant when we broke up."

149

"And that was your spiral to rock bottom?"

"Straight into hell."

When the coffee pot was full, Bruce took down two mugs and filled them. Walking to the table, he set them down, and pulled out a chair. Alex moved to take the seat across from him.

"So what will you do?"

Alex wrapped his hands around the mug. "If it's a match, and I'm her father, I guess I'll go get her. If I'd known about her, I would have already been involved in taking care of her. As it is, I'm absolutely in shock. I'm not even sure I've held a baby. I don't know the first thing about taking care of one. I'm at a loss."

Bruce nodded slowly. "Ray can help. He knows what to do. Your mom will help. And I'm here. Our own rendition of *Three Men and a Baby*, only there are two of us."

That warranted a chuckle from Alex, but then the somber worry surfaced again. "And what about Catherine? I lose her forever."

"She needs to process this. I imagine she's in a state of shock too. Up until yesterday, she assumed she'd mother your children."

That's what Alex thought too. "She took off to go to Rachel's," he said as the back door opened and Craig walked through.

"Yeah, that's why I'm here. She needs some time. You look like shit," Craig said.

"I feel like it."

"Rach says Catherine is pretty upset."

Alex let out a sigh. "Seems to be going around."

Craig walked to the cupboard and pulled down a mug. He filled it with coffee, and leaned back against the counter. "Give her some time. She'll come around."

"I don't think she will."

"She loves you. Love is powerful."

"I'm not sure it's this powerful." Alex raked his fingers through his hair. "I'll take a test tomorrow," he filled Craig in on the detail. "But the timeline matches up."

"Shit."

"Yeah, shit."

A moment later the backdoor opened again, and Ray and Toby walked into the tiny kitchen. They didn't say anything, but moved in to pour themselves coffee.

Alex looked round the room. These were his brothers, and they were all standing in the little kitchen to surround him with their love and support. Oh how different it would have been a year ago if he'd had them with him in Boston.

For the first time since the officer had arrived at the house, Alex felt a sense of calm. These men would never let him down. Something deep down inside of him told him they'd be there when he brought his daughter home, and that too was something he seemed to know was true. Alex Burke's world was about to turn upside down for the third time in a year, all because of a woman. Only this time, when he brought her home, she wasn't going to leave—not this woman.

He was getting ahead of himself. Tomorrow he'd go take the test, and then he'd wait. Regardless of the results, his life was about to change.

CHAPTER 35

*A*lex had slept in his own bed for the first time in a month. His text messages and phone calls went unanswered.

Rachel had called him when she knew Catherine was safely home. "She needs some time to process this," she'd said.

"So do I, Rach."

"She's embarrassed and feeling petty. When Catherine gets it in her head that something is so bad, it's hard for her to come around."

Alex had an entire argument, but he'd had to remember that it was Rachel on the other end of the phone and not Catherine. But the night alone had only intensified that argument in his head. He had a lot to say, but more than anything he just wanted to hold her.

Alex had driven to the location they had given him to do the DNA test. He'd never felt so sick in his entire life.

The process had been quick and painless, a simple swab to the cheek. Now, he'd wait.

As he drove back home, having taken a personal day, he'd

called the contact in Baltimore to let them know he'd taken the test.

"Mr. Burke," the woman on the other end of the phone said, "there has been another man that has come forth and he claims that the baby is his."

"But my name is on the birth certificate."

"Yes, that's always at the mother's discretion, and in this case she put your name down."

"So he wasn't around when the baby was born?"

"I don't have that information," the woman said.

"What happens now?"

"He too will need to submit a DNA sample for a paternity test. I will be in touch with the lab and should have the results within the next few days. I will call you either way."

He thanked the woman and disconnected the call. The strangest stirring of emotions swam inside of him. He might not be the baby's father after all. It might had all just been a mistake or maybe something was wrong with this other man that would make Cara not put his name down.

The emotion that he struggled with the most was the sense of loss. For the past two days he'd known the baby was his—or assumed as much. What would happen if she was the other man's daughter? Would things just go back to normal?

No, nothing about what happened was normal. And even if the baby wasn't his, there was a lot of emotional baggage to unpack. Catherine hadn't been able to stand by his side. She'd panicked.

It had only been a day, but Alex missed her. He understood that she needed her time, but he needed her.

Instead of driving out of town, he circled back to the construction lot where Ray had his offices. He pulled into the lot, but he didn't see her car.

Alex parked and stepped out of his car just as Ray and another man walked out of the front door.

"Hey," Ray said, and then excused himself from the man and walked toward Alex. "What are you doing here?"

"I was looking for Catherine, but I don't see her car."

"No, she called in today. I told her to take as much time as she needed. What did you find out?"

Alex shrugged. "I did the test. They have to process it." He ran his hands over his hair. "Another guy stepped up and said the baby was his."

"You're off the hook?"

"No. They'll get a test from both of us."

"This sucks."

"It does. I'll get out of your hair," Alex retreated from him.

"You call me if you need anything," Ray called after him. "Anything," he repeated.

ONCE ALEX LEFT RAY'S, IT WAS AUTOPILOT TO DRIVE TO Catherine's. He needed her. Yes, she was being selfish. Yes, it hurt. But right at that moment, he needed the security she offered him.

Alex parked in the driveway. At least if she wanted to leave it would stop her from backing out with his car there. He opted to not use his key, instead he stood on the front step, as he had so many times before, and rang the bell.

He heard the movement inside the house, and a moment later Catherine pulled open the door. She was in a bathrobe. Her hair fell over her face and looked as if it hadn't been brushed in days. Her skin was blotchy and her eyes red. This wasn't what he'd expected at all and it twisted him up.

Catherine stood in the doorway, still holding the door as if she might shut it on him.

"What are you doing here? Why aren't you at work?" she asked.

"I had things I had to do. Ray said you called in. Are you okay?"

"Do I look okay?"

No. He'd never seen anyone look worse, and yet she was still the most beautiful woman he'd ever known.

"Can I come in? I want to be with you," he said inching toward the door.

"I'm kinda wallowing in my own self-pity right now."

He couldn't help but smile at that. Hadn't Rachel mentioned that?

"Maybe we can wallow together."

Catherine took a moment before stepping back and letting him in. As she shut the door, Alex turned to her, and gently he took her hand. At least the ring was still on her finger, and he took that as a good sign.

"I miss you," he said.

"You were with me yesterday morning."

"It seems like a long time ago." He eased closer to her. "Do you want to talk about it?"

Catherine pursed her lips. "Not really."

"We can't just let it go. Things changed the other day."

"And I'm petty enough to have taken it personally."

Alex lifted his hand to her cheek and caressed it gently. "It's personal. It was a blow to you."

"What about you? Did you even think something like this…"

"No," he cut her off. "I never could have imagined something like this. Not after the way things ended between me and Cara."

Catherine rested her hands on his chest. "Did you love her?"

"No," he said without thinking about it. "I never loved her."

"But when she left, look what happened to you."

"It wasn't that she left," he admitted, gathering her hands in his and holding them between them. "It was the string of lies and the betrayal that caused me to go down that hole. Maybe I thought it was love then, but I know now it wasn't. Nothing with her was close to what I feel with you."

"And what do you know about the baby."

"I know that I turned in my DNA and another man has said the baby is his."

Catherine's eyes went wide. "So all of this might be a mistake?"

"It could be, but listen to me," he began as he pressed kisses to her fingers. "The timeline lines up, Cath." He took a breath. "This baby might be mine, and I can't do it alone. If the test comes back, and I'm her father, I have to give her a good life."

Catherine's sad eyes looked up into his as she lifted her hands to his cheeks, and moved in to gently kiss him. As she eased back, tears streamed down her cheeks. "I don't know if I can be a part of that."

CHAPTER 36

*A*lex had walked out of Catherine's house Monday morning, and had driven home, sat on the couch, and he didn't move. He didn't turn on the TV. He didn't open the beer he had sitting on the table next to him. Eventually the room grew dark, and he still sat there.

When a voice broke the silence, he wasn't surprised. But when it was his sister's voice, he began to sob. A moment later Sarah's hand came to his shoulder.

"Catherine called. She thought I should come check on you," she said as she walked around the end table to sit next to him on the couch. "She's worried about you."

"I can't imagine that's what she feels."

"Just because she can't do this, it doesn't mean she doesn't love you."

Alex let out a snort. "I think love should be what makes her want to be here with me. And wouldn't it be nice if I knew for sure?"

Sarah sat back, resting her head to the back of the couch. "What are you going to do?"

"If it comes back that she's mine, I'm bringing her home."

"You're sure?"

"I'm sure."

Sarah reached for his hand and gave it a squeeze. "Okay then. I'm going to be here. I'll sleep on the couch until things are settled. I'll spend my days off with her while you work or get stuff done. I'll do laundry. I'll…"

Alex pulled his sister to him and sobbed on her shoulder. That was what he wanted from Catherine.

"It's going to be okay," she whispered in his ear. "If she's yours, I'll be packed and ready to go with you to get her."

And at that moment, he knew his life had completely shifted, but he would forever love Catherine. That would be a heartbreak he was just going to have to learn to live with.

WEDNESDAY AFTERNOON SARAH PULLED OPEN THE BACK DOOR, HER arms were filled with bags of food. Alex sat at the table, his phone wrapped in his hands. He'd forgotten she was going to bring dinner. Hell, after the phone call he'd just taken, he wasn't even sure what day it was.

Sarah set the bags on the counter and turned to Alex. "Are you okay?"

"I'm not sure," he said softly.

"You're freaking me out," Sarah said as she pulled out the chair next to him and sat down. "Something is wrong. What happened?"

"I just got a call from the state of Maryland. The other man who claimed that the baby was his, they received his test back."

"His DNA?"

Alex nodded. "He's not the baby's father."

"What does that mean?"

"They got my test back too."

Sarah reached for his hands and grasped them in hers. "And?"

He lifted his eyes to hers. The emotions swirling inside of him made him dizzy. "It appears I have a five-month old daughter named Celia Rose."

THE NEXT MORNING SARAH AND ALEX WERE ON AN AIRPLANE bound for Baltimore. He had a meeting with the state representative that afternoon. He had no idea what to expect. All he knew was he would be flying home with his infant daughter, and he knew nothing about being a father.

He'd been assured that most new parents didn't know anything about parenting, but most of them had had time to consider it. In his case, it was a complete surprise. There hadn't been time to get her a crib or necessities. Sarah had promised to stay with him, and for that he was more than grateful.

It would work out, he told himself over and over.

The moment they had told him his paternity test was a positive match, everything he'd been thinking up to that moment changed. Life had been all about him and what he wanted out of it. Now he knew someone else was dependent on him, and it was suddenly all about her—Celia Rose.

Having not slept much the night before, he kept telling himself to nap on the plane, but he couldn't. His mind raced with thoughts about what she looked like. Would she resemble him or Cara? Had Cara done drugs or drank? He was sure he could rule that out. She might have been a little lose on her morals, for having been in what he thought was a committed relationship, but she never was much of a drinker and as far as he'd known had never done drugs.

What would he tell Celia Rose about her mother when the day came? He let out a breath. He'd have to work on that, and he figured he had years to put that together. Alex and Cara had been together for years, surely he could see past the blinding anger and grief that she'd caused him and build a mother worthy of their daughter.

Then the thought struck him. Would Celia Rose ever have a mother?

Alex squeezed his eyes shut tightly. This wasn't how he'd planned his life, but it sure as hell would have been nicer to have Catherine be part of it.

The thought put an ache in his chest. He loved her—God he loved her. He never would have taken her for the petty person she was proving to be. Then again, this was a pretty big order to expect someone to take on.

Maybe she just needed some time.

He opened his eyes and looked out the window to his side. No, she knew she couldn't be part of the life he was about to take on. That was her right, and he couldn't hold it against her.

Alex's reality now was that he was a father. Celia Rose needed him, and it was a forever commitment, and one he would have made a year ago had Cara told him about her.

He closed his eyes again and willed himself to sleep. Everything now was about Celia Rose. Catherine Anderson was going to have to just become a memory.

*a*lex hadn't expected to walk into the building, tell them his name, and get his daughter—well, maybe he had.

There were forms. There were questions. And then there were background checks, which would take another day. A hearing was scheduled for the next morning to assure that he wanted custody of his own child. But he'd hoped to see his daughter, but that wasn't in the schedule for the day.

A meeting was arranged for the following morning when the foster care providers would bring the baby to him after the hearing. At that time, if everything aligned correctly, he'd have his daughter with him and he could take her back home. There was also the chance that he'd have to stick around in Baltimore a little longer, but he was ready to do that.

The case wasn't in the state's care because he'd been neglectful. If he'd known about Celia Rose, he'd never have left Boston. He'd probably have followed Cara wherever she'd ended up.

Guilt twisted with the nerves. Had he ignored her when she tried to tell him?

Alex was sick with the nervous energy it all brought on. He'd met people over the years, and even a few celebrities here and there, and yet, knowing he'd see Celia Rose for the first time, he couldn't believe how nervous he was.

Sarah sat at the table in their hotel room, absentmindedly eating chips from a bag. She'd been texting Rachel all day and working on gathering information using his laptop.

"Okay, what I've learned is this," she said looking up at him and pulling the laptop to her lap. "The information they gave you says that Celia Rose was being breastfed by her mother. After the accident, she had supplemented breast milk from a donor."

"I didn't even know that was a thing."

"Yep," Sarah said as she took another chip. "There are banks, like food banks, if you will, for breast milk. I have a list of them in Denver. There are also boards online where people post that they have milk to donate."

"And I have to know this right now, don't I?"

Sarah nodded. "You do." She stood and carried the laptop over to the bed where he'd been trying to rest his eyes. She sat down next to him and showed him the list. "You can decide to wean her off the breast milk if you want. But, breast milk is better for her."

Alex rubbed his eyes. "Go on."

"Rachel is picking up some diapers, bottles, a warmer, and a few clothes and blankets. We figured just enough to get you through the first week. Then you'll know if she spits up a lot, or poops excessively, or…"

"Shit."

"Babies are huge responsibilities. There's a lot of stuff here. Had you known she was coming, you'd have had nine months to prepare. You have like nine hours."

"I get it. I've never even changed a baby."

"I have experience from my babysitting days. Mom has experience from her mom days," she laughed. "Alex, no one knows what they're doing right away. You'll have a rhythm in a week."

"I don't know."

"I do. You're a caretaker. You've always been one. Celia Rose is in good hands. And her auntie is going to be there as much as you need. I'm not going to let you do this alone."

"Thank you."

"You'll owe me."

And didn't he know it? "Speaking of Mom…"

"She's fine. She's more mad that you didn't know."

"Me too. Now I wonder if she tried to tell me."

"If so, she should have tried harder." Sarah picked up the computer and carried it back to the table when a noise came from it. "Do you know a John Kramer?"

The name made Alex wince. "Yeah."

"He just messaged you through your Facebook app," she said, carrying the computer back over to him and handing it to him. "Who is he?"

"Oh, in the end, he's the piece of shit Cara took off with. Former co-worker and friend, I thought. But one of her many conquests," he bit out the words as he sat up and took the computer from his sister. "As if I need this right now."

Alex scooted back on the bed so that his back was against the headboard. He scrolled through the screens until he found his app, and looked at the message.

Hey Alex,

I'm probably the last person you expected to hear from, or would want to. I'm in Baltimore and I hear you're coming this way. I would like to meet you and talk. It's about Celia Rose.

Breast milk, diapers, spit-up, and poop didn't seem to overwhelm him now at all. But he thought he might just get sick thinking about the man behind the message. What did he have to tell him about Celia Rose? The man had double-crossed him more than once, and if he was the other man claiming she was his, well Alex had won that battle—or in the moment that's how he saw it.

It has to be tonight. I'm in the downtown area. Where and when?

The message was curt, but Alex really didn't care. Luckily

Sarah would be with him, because he wasn't sure he could control his anger around the man.

To his face, John had been a pal. They'd worked together, played basketball on weekends, and in the end, he'd been carrying on with Cara behind Alex's back. It was his name on her lips the day she'd walked out. And it was the name in Alex's head the first night he'd blacked out after drinking.

Eight o'clock. O'Malley's?

Alex did a quick search for the name. It was a restaurant with a bar only six blocks away. That would work.

I'll be there. My sister is coming with me to hear whatever you have to say about Celia Rose.

Before Alex could close the laptop, John replied.

I'll meet you there.

CHAPTER 38

The empty pint of ice cream sat on the coffee table, the spoon inside. There was a bag of chips open, and crumbs on the floor. A bottle of wine sat open on the floor, next to the couch.

Catherine sipped from the glass, and numbed herself.

She ignored the pounding at the front door, and Rachel's incessant calling of her name. "You know I have a key. Why don't you just open the door?"

Catherine picked up the bottle from the floor, and with her glass in her hand, she carefully stood and walked to the door. Flipping the lock, she walked away toward the kitchen.

Rachel pushed the door open the moment Catherine had stepped away.

"This is ridiculous. What are you doing?"

"I'm wallowing in self-pity," she said, sitting down at the kitchen table, because she couldn't walk any further.

"I've never seen you so pathetic."

"I guess it's my turn. I've seen you this low many times."

Rachel nodded and took the bottle from her. "You sure have. Maybe I should find you a facility to go to and recover."

Catherine narrowed her eyes. "I deserve this."

"You do. You know what, you absolutely do," Rachel set the bottle back down, and then sat in the chair across from Catherine. "Ray said you haven't been to work all week."

"He said to take as much time as I need. I needed it," her words slurred.

"I can't believe you're acting like this."

"Like what? Like a woman who lost the man she loved?"

"Like a woman who gave up on the man she loved. This is all you. You haven't even given a moment's thought to what he's going through right now."

Catherine drank down the wine in her glass. "He has a baby." The tears began and she tried to wipe them away as quickly as they fell. "He has a baby."

Rachel pulled Catherine to her and held her. "Sweetheart, let it out."

Catherine let the tears roll onto Rachel's shoulder as Rachel ran her hand over Catherine's back.

The sobs grew harder until Catherine almost couldn't breathe. "I hate myself for this."

"I get it."

"I want to be happy for him. I want to understand. I can't." She sat back and wiped her eyes on the arms of her robe. "Have you talked to him?"

"I talked to Sarah."

"Does he have her?" Catherine asked as she refilled her wine.

Rachel watched her carefully as she drank down the wine. "Not yet. They're in Maryland. Probably tomorrow."

"Well, that's that." Catherine looked down at her hand, twisted the ring on her finger, and then took it off.

"What are you doing?"

"I don't need this anymore."

Rachel slapped her hands down on the table and picked up

the bottle again. This time she stood and carried it to the sink to pour out the little that was left.

"I can't believe you. You are the most selfish woman I have ever known."

Catherine wanted to stand, but her head swam from the wine she'd already consumed. "Screw you!" she shouted. "Look at what happened to you when Craig disappeared after college. Hell, you tried to take your own life. I'm just throwing a fit."

"I don't know why I bother with you."

"Because I was by your side for all of it," Catherine reminded her and then felt the sting of her own words. "Besides, are you here fighting for me or Alex?"

"At this moment..." she'd stopped, but Catherine didn't need to hear it. And deep in her heart she knew she was fighting for both of them, but Catherine knew she was being selfish.

Catherine pushed the glass away and ran her hand over her face, wiping away tears. "What's her name?"

"Celia Rose."

Catherine's lips trembled. "That's pretty."

"I'm gathering some things for them for when they return."

"That's generous of you."

She saw the wince on Rachel's face. There would be more words between them. This argument would go round and round. Yet Catherine couldn't see clearly enough yet to just let it all go.

Rachel rubbed her hands over her belly. "Why don't you go get a shower and go with me. Help me buy the stuff they need. I get that you can't wrap your head around all of this, but..."

"No," Catherine said, the tears stinging her eyes again. "I can't do that."

Disappointment was clearly worn on Rachel's face. "Then I'll go. I don't know when I'll be back by. Make sure you take that shower and show up to work on Monday. It would be horribly disappointing if you let everyone down."

Catherine knew she deserved that. Managing to stand,

Catherine walked to the cupboard and pulled an envelope out from under the plates.

"Here," she handed it to Rachel.

"What is this?"

"An emergency fund, if you will. Use it to buy her a crib, or something that they'll need."

Rachel held it back toward her. "You do it."

Catherine shook her head. "No. This is what I can do for now. I know he has a long road ahead of him. Celia Rose will be in good hands. He'll be an amazing father."

Rachel looked at the envelope and back at Catherine. Then, what Catherine knew was a nervous habit, Rachel lifted her fingers to her shoulder and rubbed at the scar that was there, where she'd been shot only a few months earlier.

Catherine squeezed her eyes tight. God, Rachel could bring a baby into the world with the man she fought for, and she could ward off the horrible things that had happened to her, and yet Catherine couldn't help herself against the pettiness.

"I love you, Cath. I really do," Rachel said. "I wish you'd come around to this. He's in pain. He needs you."

Catherine had to look away from her dearest friend in the world. She was letting everyone she loved down, but her heart hurt so badly, she just couldn't help it.

CHAPTER 39

*a*lex opened the door to O'Malley's and let his sister walk
in before him. The bar was to their left, and he had to
assume that was where John Kramer would be.

Alex looked around and found the man at a high top table in
the corner. At least he'd understood Alex was bringing his sister
as it was a table for three.

He walked toward the table where the man looked lost in his
drink. "John."

When the man lifted his eyes, they were weary. But he smiled.
"Hey, Alex. It's really nice to see you."

When John's gaze shifted behind Alex, he turned and reached
for his sister's hand. "This is my sister, Sarah."

John didn't extend his hand, but he smiled again. "It's nice to
meet you."

Alex and Sarah took their seats.

"Order whatever you like," John said. "Jack and Coke, right?"

The mention of the drink made Alex want to puke. "Not
anymore. I'm fine. I really just want to hear what you have to
say."

John shook the glass in front of him, making the ice clink, before taking a sip and setting it back down.

"Alright. I moved to Baltimore with Cara in December. By then I knew she was pregnant." He rubbed a finger over his brows. "I knew, but she never really told me. There was never a discussion about, *hey I'm pregnant*," he said waving a hand in the air. "I assumed from the start it was my baby. She," he corrected. "But Cara was further along than I knew."

"She left me in October to be with you."

John nodded, his nose crinkled up. "Man, I am so sorry. I mean…"

"Water under the bridge and not something I care much to discuss. She never told me she was pregnant."

"She found out after she'd left you. She thought she was just stressed. Who wouldn't be after what she did to us?" John said as if Cara's betrayal went deeper than what she'd done to Alex. "Word got around pretty quickly the path you went down. The drinking. You losing your job." John took another sip. "She was scared."

"I never touched her."

"I know that. She'd messed up. She was embarrassed, and then she found out she was pregnant."

"What a grand secret to keep," Alex spat out the words.

"She tried to tell you," John said, lifting his cup and swirling the ice again. "She called for days."

Alex winced, and pushed back the tears that stung his eyes. "I erased all of her messages. I didn't want anything to do with her."

John nodded. "She knew that when you didn't return her calls. By then, we'd moved here. She didn't tell me the baby was yours until right before she was born. I thought maybe something was wrong, you know, she was two months further than I thought she should be in size. Then she told me she'd been pregnant since August. That messed up my timeline."

"It's hard to love a woman who can't tell you the truth," Alex said, and then his mind went right to Catherine. At least she had no problem with the truth, no matter how distasteful it might be.

"I left. I moved in with a friend, and she went on with her life. Celia Rose was born May eighth." John drank down the rest of his drink and let out a breath. "I went to the hospital to visit her. Looking at her, I knew she was your baby. The moment she was born, she looked like you."

"Then why challenge the paternity?"

"I had to know for sure."

Alex nodded. He supposed he understood that. "I could have pieced this all together. Why am I here?"

John reached into his pocket and pulled out a key. "Her dad and I have been talking. He's nearly eighty and they weren't very close after Cara's mother died. He'd like you to keep him updated on Celia Rose. I'll send you his address." John tapped the key. "This is the key to the apartment we shared, before I moved out. Her dad asked me to clean it out. I thought maybe you'd like to go through there with me and take what belongs to Celia Rose."

Alex's jaw trembled so he gritted his teeth together. "I don't..."

"She was a good mom. A lousy human, but a good mom," John assured him. "She was scrapbooking everything. At least ship back the clothes and supplies she had on hand. Take the pictures and gifts that she'd received. It'll give you a starting point to see Celia Rose's life, and you can have something for her, for when she gets older."

Alex hadn't considered that he'd gain anything out of their meeting, but John was right. At least he'd have something for Celia Rose when she got older.

"If everything goes according to plan, I'll have her tomorrow."

"There's no reason for them not to give her to you. You're a good man. She should have been with you the whole time."

And Alex took that on himself. If Cara had tried, and he'd backed away, there had to be a point she stopped trying to include him.

"I appreciate this," Alex said. "Will you just meet me at her place? I don't want to take the key and go myself."

John nodded. "Yeah, just let me know when. I'll be there."

Alex nodded. "I guess I'll go back and get my last night of good sleep," he said as he stood from the stool, and Sarah did the same. "Thanks again."

As they turned, John called after him. "Hey, the grapevine is pretty big. I hear you're getting married. Congrats." John held up his empty glass, and Sarah reached for Alex's hand, and gave it a tight squeeze.

There would be no sleep tonight, he thought.

CHAPTER 40

*A*lex had been right. He hadn't gotten a wink of sleep all night. A million things ran through his head keeping him awake.

He thought of his relationship with Cara. What had he really thought of it? They'd been together for years, well, on and off. It had been a volatile relationship, but it had been a relationship. They'd moved in with each other a year before she'd walked out —before he'd told her to pack her sorry ass and leave.

He hadn't missed her, he thought in the dark. He'd never missed her at all. The drinking and the self-loathing was all on him. The life he'd ended up with wasn't the one he'd planned. He was thousands of miles from home, in a job that had lost its appeal, and the woman he thought he'd loved, had lied to him and cheated.

Alex pounded the pillow under his head, and turned to his side. He missed Catherine.

It hadn't even been a week since he'd learned about Celia Rose, but he felt as if in gaining her, he'd lost everything.

He was going to have to take a leave from work, for a few

weeks at least, until he knew how to handle things. There was enough in his savings for that. But he wanted to share this with Catherine. How did he not know she could be so petty?

Then again, that was a big order to assume someone would want to take on a child, born to another woman, and make her her own.

When had his life become some out of control soap opera?

The alarm on his phone went off, and he groaned. So much for getting one more night of rest before his entire life changed.

Sarah opened the door to the room, and Alex sat up in the bed. Well, somewhere he must have fallen asleep. He hadn't even heard her leave.

"I brought some coffee and some breakfast. This is a big day," her voice was filled with optimism and delight. He wasn't sure he was ready for that.

"When did you leave?"

"Six o'clock. You were tossing and turning all night. I thought you could use something to fuel you. I also ordered up a crib for tonight."

Rubbing his eyes, he smiled. "Thanks for doing all of this."

"I'm giddy. I woke up anxious to hold my niece."

Perhaps her positivity was just what he needed. He was a few hours from holding his daughter. The thought caused him to suck in a breath and nearly choke on it.

As if the past week hadn't been full of realizations. He thought about it again. He was a father. He was about to meet his daughter, and hadn't John said she looked just like Alex?

"Are you okay? You don't look well," Sarah handed him the coffee from the tray.

"I just realized I'm meeting my daughter soon."

She laughed. "Just realized it?"

"It's just been information thrown at me. But I'm going to hold her."

Sarah smiled. "It might have not been ideal, but I'm so excited for you. You're going to be an amazing dad."

"Thanks. I wish Catherine were here," he said and for the first time he saw anger cloud his sister's eyes.

"Her loss," she spat out the words. "Sorry. But, no I'm not," she sat down on the bed across from him. "I'm mad. I'd say if she loved you, but she does love you. Her attitude is pure bullshit. If something bad happened to her, you'd be there. Hell, look at all the support she gave Rachel when she went down that dark hole, and even when she and Craig got back together and she was shot. She couldn't look past the logistics of this and support you?"

He knew he was staring, and he didn't know if he should cheer on her anger or laugh.

Instead, he smiled. "Thanks." Alex wrapped his hands around his cup. "I'm trying to be very understanding about it. Isn't it always the man that runs? I suppose women get scared too."

Sarah shook her head. "You love her too much to be mad, don't you?"

"I'm hurt. But Celia Rose needs me."

"Catherine's loss. She will never truly know how amazing a man you are." Sarah stood and bent to kiss him on the cheek.

Family, he thought as she moved to pull food from the bag she'd carried in. Family would always have your back, even if that family was made up of friends. Wasn't Rachel back home making sure things were ready for Celia Rose when they got back? Hadn't all his *brothers* sat in his kitchen and supported him?

No doubt they were supporting Catherine too.

He let out a breath. Their lives would forever be intertwined, he thought. With or without her, he had his friends, and they were her friends too. And he'd have Celia Rose.

Catherine would either have to lay low forever, or she'd have to accept his daughter was part of his life. Maybe she'd come around, but maybe she wouldn't.

He had to stop worrying about it. At the moment, he needed to wake up, fuel up, and get ready.

He was about to meet the woman who had his heart, and he hadn't even laid eyes on her yet. Already he knew he loved Celia Rose more than anyone in the world—including Catherine.

CHAPTER 41

*a*lex wondered if there was a certain heart rate that wasn't healthy. His hammered in his chest as they'd sat him and Sarah in a room alone.

When he held his hands out, they shook. Had he ever been so nervous in all his life?

Sarah reached for him, laying her hand on his arm. "Breathe."

"I can't."

She laughed as she pulled out her cell phone. "I'm going to document all of this. You're going to sob."

"Thanks for the encouragement."

"You're going to meet your own flesh and blood. You're a daddy."

Alex scrubbed his shaking hands over his face. God he was glad he'd brought his sister with him. "I love you. Thank you."

"Give me your phone too."

He laughed as he handed it to her. "Why?"

"I'm going to face-time Mom. She should see this."

And this was what it was all about.

Sarah managed to get their mother on the phone, and poise

the other phone on a bookshelf in the room so that it recorded, before the door opened.

When it did, Alex rose to his feet as the court liaison he'd been working with walked through. "Are you ready?"

Alex sucked in another breath, and reached for his sister's hand. "I'm ready."

He held his breath as another woman walked in with the baby on her shoulder. She was asleep.

Alex pressed his hand to his mouth. All he could see was dark hair and the large pink bow headband they had on her. He'd yet to even see her face, but feeling her presence in the room stirred up every emotion he'd ever had.

Tears streamed over his cheeks, and he brushed them away with his free hand. He could hear his sister sobbing, and his mother too.

The woman holding her, cradled her, and it was the first moment he saw her face.

The tears fell harder now. He had no idea love could be so instant.

"Daddy, this is Celia Rose," the woman said as she handed the sleeping infant to him.

Alex dropped his sister's hand and reached his arms out. The woman laid Celia Rose in his arms, and he instantly felt his knees go weak. With his sister's hand on his back, he sat back down on the couch.

He could hear his mother's sobs on the phone. "Alex, she's beautiful," she said as Sarah held the phone up.

Alex wanted to speak. He wanted to say something, but he was speechless. All he could do was look at her.

When she started to stir, she opened her eyes and looked up at him. He knew in that moment she knew him.

Gently he lifted her to his shoulder, smelling the softness of her, and he kissed her on the cheek. He'd never in his life had a moment so pure. It didn't matter that Cara was her mother and that Catherine wasn't. Alex was her daddy, and Celia Rose was with him now.

~

THEY'D STAYED IN THE ROOM WITH CELIA ROSE AND HER FOSTER mother for over an hour as she talked him through the past week of Celia Rose's life. She'd assured him that she was a good and calm baby. He'd had his first opportunity to change a diaper, and they'd set him up with a cooler of breast milk that would get him home.

Sarah had already contacted Rachel to work on getting donated milk back home.

They had taken her back to the hotel, and Alex watched as his sister and his daughter bonded. He had no idea he'd needed Celia Rose in his life.

The judge had the paperwork in hand to file Celia Rose's new last name, and John had texted him the address and the time to meet him.

Alex opted to leave Celia Rose with Sarah, and go by himself.

John was in the apartment when he arrived. It wasn't much of a place to live. In fact, it surprised Alex that she'd chosen to live there with the baby.

"We didn't have much when we moved here," John said. "It was all we could find. I moved in with a buddy after we broke up. She stayed."

Alex circled around the living room. The plants were dying, there were still dishes in the sink, and the trash had never been taken out. The thought struck him right in the chest, Cara hadn't intended on never returning.

He knew she was dead, but the magnitude of it hit him, and he had to sit down.

"She's buried in Boston," John said. "Her funeral was on Wednesday."

Alex hadn't even thought to ask about that. His entire focus had been on getting to Celia Rose. "I'm sorry, I didn't think to ask about funeral plans."

John nodded. "It was a small ceremony. Her dad didn't want a lot of people."

"I'd stay and help you clean this out, but..."

"You need to get back to your life." John sat down in a chair across from him. "I'll never be able to apologize for what we did to you," he said looking down at his clasped hands. "We both lied to your face. I've never done that to anyone before, and God, I hope no one ever does that to me."

"It's in the past. I have a lot more to worry about."

John nodded again. "What does your fiancée think about all of this?"

Did he really want to get into this with the man? Alex sighed. "I'm not sure of the fiancée status at the moment. This was a lot to take in."

"If she gets to meet Celia Rose, she'll change her mind. She might only be a few months old, but she's got a powerful presence."

And hadn't Alex felt that the moment he'd held her? "What is Celia Rose's? I should get it packed up and sent home."

"Right." John stood. "I made a pile of photos that she had around the apartment. There are a few with her in them. I didn't know if you wanted those."

"I'll take them. She deserves to know who her mother was."

"I agree. I hope you don't mind. I took the few that had me in them. She let me come by a few times after Celia Rose was born. I think I wanted to be part of it, but she was done with me."

Alex didn't know what to think of that either. It was an interesting turn of events, he felt sorry for John, but he had to stay focused.

John picked up a scrapbook and handed it to him. "She'd kept it current up to the past few weeks. It kept her calm," he said.

"She wrote about you in there too and added some pictures. I guess she was prepared to make sure you were part of her life."

Alex didn't want to break down in front of the man. He just needed to get out of there.

John walked to the bedroom. There was a bed, which hadn't been made, and a bassinet next to the bed. He wasn't sure where she would have put a full crib if she'd had one.

"Her clothes are in the drawer. I brought up a few boxes for you."

"I appreciate that," Alex said as she stepped into the room, which still smelled of Cara's perfume. "I'll only be a few minutes."

"If I'm ever in Colorado, I'd like to stop in and see you both. Again, you were a good friend. I'm so sorry."

Alex watched as John turned and walked out of the room.

CHAPTER 42

"I shipped the boxes to the house, but they'll arrive sometime next week. They gave us enough breast milk to get home with," Alex said as he talked to Rachel using the speaker on the phone, and changed Celia Rose's diaper while Sarah packed up.

"I have already talked to the milk bank. They are holding milk for me, and I'll go pick it up in a few hours. We have everything you need here for her. I can't wait to meet her."

"You're going to fall in love," Alex said as he lifted his daughter to his shoulder and she cooed in his ear. "I'm smitten," he added.

"I can hear it in your voice. We'll all try not to overwhelm you, but we can't wait to see her."

"And Catherine?" he had to ask, and when his sister turned to look at him, he saw the disappointment in her eyes.

"Alex…"

"I know, Rach. I had to ask."

"I've never seen her act like this. It's as if she's turned into a selfish five-year-old. I just want to throw something at her." He heard the tension in her voice.

"We all take stressful news differently. This isn't exactly how I'd expected my week to end. But, Rach," he kissed Celia Rose's head, "I'm so in love. She's the best thing to ever happen to me. I didn't know I'd feel this way."

"Hurry home. I can't wait."

~

COLORADO OFTEN GRACED HER RESIDENTS WITH BEAUTIFUL weather, even in October, and Catherine was going to take full advantage of it.

She'd called Ray after she'd taken her shower, and apologized for having missed the week. It was unprofessional, selfish, and would never happen again.

With her hair atop her head, she opened the windows, stripped the bed of sheets, and began cleaning.

There was a need to purge herself of the week she'd had wallowing in her self-pity. She'd gone days between showers.

She'd drank four bottles of wine, and eaten everything she could possibly find in a bag, but in the end, she hadn't had anything of nutritional value.

There had been some curt and mean texts sent to Rachel, which she hadn't really remembered sending, but there was proof on her phone.

If their friendship was as strong as it always had been, Rachel wouldn't hold them against her. But she couldn't blame her if she did.

Catherine was embarrassed, but she was also in mourning.

Her engagement ring still sat on the kitchen table, where she'd taken it off. When she felt emotionally stable enough, she'd take it back to Alex. She was sure he could buy something for the baby if he were to sell it.

Catherine began scrubbing every bathroom, cleaning every

floor, and vacuuming. It was while she was vacuuming that she missed the text that Rachel sent.

They land in twenty minutes. We're all going over to the house to see the baby. You should come see your contribution and meet his daughter.

When she didn't reply, Rachel sent another text.

You're being a selfish bitch. You should hear him talk about her. You're missing out on something beautiful. But if that's who you want to be...

By the time Catherine had noticed the texts hours later, she was angry, hurt, and conflicted. And as she held her phone in her hands another text came through from Rachel. *I'm sorry. I love you. Nachos and drinks on Thursday. I'll buy. Let's get back to normal.*

Catherine set down her phone, picked it back up, and turned it off. She needed some normal back, but for a few more days, she needed silence.

❧

ALEX LAUGHED AS HE PULLED UP IN FRONT OF THE HOUSE. THIS was what he got when he'd put Rachel in charge of getting everything they needed for Celia Rose.

Sarah was crying in the back seat. "Oh, God! Look at that."

The front walk was lined with pink balloons, and there was a cut-out of a stork in the grass. A handmade sign hung in the front window that said, WELCOME HOME, CELIA ROSE.

Instead of pulling all the way into the garage, he parked so that they would go in through the front door.

The street was lined with the familiar cars of their friends. He hadn't expected this kind of homecoming. And he couldn't help but look for Catherine's car, but it wasn't there.

Sarah unbuckled Celia Rose's seat, and then Alex pulled her from it. He wanted to carry her inside to meet her family.

Sarah gathered the cooler, the diaper bag the foster mother

had given them, and the empty car seat, and followed Alex to the door.

When he walked up the step, he could hear the hushed sounds from inside, and when he walked through the door, the house was full.

His mother moved to them first, rising on her toes to kiss his cheek, and then taking a moment to gaze at her granddaughter. "Hello, my Celia Rose. I'm your grandmother," she said before taking her from him and placing her on her shoulder.

The look in his mother's eyes told him that he'd done the right thing in bringing her back home. This was where Celia Rose needed to be.

Rachel moved to him and enveloped him in her arms. "Congratulations. She's beautiful," she said as Craig moved in and shook his hand.

"You beat us to it," he teased before he lowered his hand and rested it on his wife's belly.

"Who knew, huh?"

Bruce and Toby each shook his hand and hugged him, and Ray did the same as he kept a hand on each of his children who were eager to look at the new baby.

Alex noticed that a table was set up with a cake, and there were presents with Celia Rose's name on them. How could he ever thank them all enough?

The door to her bedroom was open, and Alex stepped into the pink haven, which had been an empty room when he'd left. There was a plush C and R on the wall, a rocking chair, and a crib. The crib had a rose engraved on it.

Rachel touched his shoulder. "This should get you started. And everyone brought diapers and wipes, and of course other gifts."

"Thank you. Tell me what I owe you and…"

"Nothing. Give her a good life. Besides, I didn't buy all of this."

"Everyone chipped in?" he asked.

"Yeah. Everyone," she said turning to look up at him. "The crib is from Catherine."

The thudding in his chest was back, as well as the ache. He rubbed his palm over his breast bone to ease it.

"Catherine bought the crib?"

Rachel nodded. "It's all she can do. I don't know what to say, Alex. I'm so sorry."

He pulled Rachel to him. "Not everyone can adapt like you can to a situation that is out of their control. I get her not wanting to see this through. It must be hard to know I have this, and we're not sharing it."

"You're an asshole," she said laughing through tears. "You shouldn't take the high road. You should be petty too."

"I can't be. Have you met my daughter? She's perfect."

CHAPTER 43

*C*atherine walked into the bar for her nacho and drinks date with Rachel on Thursday after work. She hadn't spoken to her since she'd received the texts, so it was entirely possible Rachel wasn't going to be there.

But, as a true friend would be, Rachel sat at the same high top they usually met at. There were nachos on the table, a margarita in front of the empty chair, and Rachel sitting with an iced tea.

"I wasn't sure you'd be here," Catherine said as she pulled out the chair and sat down.

"Why, because you never returned my text messages or my calls all week? Yeah, I can see where you might get that idea."

So, Rachel still had a bit of an attitude toward her, Catherine thought. She totally deserved it, and if she was going to keep the relationship they had intact, then she was going to sit there and take the abuse.

"Ray said you've gone back to work," Rachel lifted a chip from the platter.

"I did. He was more than gracious. I've been going in an hour early each day, and I'll work this weekend to get caught up."

"That's good." Rachel took another chip. "Craig and I are

looking at booking a vacation, before Thanksgiving. A baby-moon," she laughed. "It won't be long before I can't travel, and then with the holidays, and all…"

"Rach, are you really going to do this?"

"A babymoon? Of course. It's the hip thing to do."

"I mean, you're just going to skirt around Alex and his baby, and how mad you are at me?"

Rachel pursed her lips and then reached for her purse. She pulled out an envelope and set it on the table.

"What is this?" Catherine slid the envelope toward her.

"Just open the damn thing."

Catherine opened the envelope and pulled out the card. When she opened the card, a photo fell to the table, image side down.

She saw Alex's handwriting in the card, so she didn't pick the picture back up.

CATHERINE,

Celia Rose and I would like to thank you for the beautiful crib. It appears to be a good one, she's been sleeping for six hours at a time, and I'm told that's really good.

Most of all, I want to tell you that I love you and I miss you. This journey will never be the same without you. I hope that you're doing well, and that someday you will come meet my daughter. Above everything, I miss our friendship.

All of our love,

Alex and Celia Rose

THE CARD SHOOK IN HER HAND AND TEARS WELLED IN HER EYES. Rachel picked up her purse again and slid a small package of tissues toward her.

Catherine took the tissues, pulled one out, and wiped her eyes without looking at Rachel.

"Look at the damn picture," Rachel's words were sharp.

With shaky hands, Catherine lifted the picture from the table and turned it over. And the tears didn't well this time, they streamed down her cheeks.

Celia Rose was the most beautiful baby she'd ever laid eyes on, and the love in her daddy's eyes was evident.

Celia Rose looked up at him with a smile. Her eyes and mouth matched Alex's, as did the fine hair atop her head. A polka dot bow on top of her head only accentuated the fact that he thought she was a gift.

Rachel stood and walked around the table to pull Catherine into her arms.

"I know you're hurting," she said softly. "I wish I could make it better. You should just go see him. He wants to share this with you."

Catherine shook her head and eased back, looking back at the photo. "He deserves better. He deserves someone who didn't act like a child and who can let go."

"It would have been easier if he'd cheated and this happened, right?"

Catherine wiped her eyes and laughed. "I think it would have been. My anger would have been justified. Me being angry because he did what was right for a daughter he didn't know about, it's stupid."

Rachel wiped Catherine's cheeks with the back of her hand. "Then pull up your big girl panties and just go meet her. I'm not saying stay and get married. I'm saying, as a friend, support him since you know he did the right thing. Seriously, you're making me reconsider you as a babysitter," Rachel teased and Catherine laughed again.

As Rachel took her seat, and the waitress refilled her tea, Catherine looked at the picture of Alex and Celia Rose. She was beautiful, and looked just like her beaming father. He deserved this happiness, and he deserved not to even think about how

Catherine felt about it. Maybe she'd work up the courage to go see him—maybe.

For that moment, she was going to drink her margarita and eat nachos with her pregnant friend.

"Where are you thinking of going for your babymoon?"

CHAPTER 44

Sarah had convinced Alex to go to the YMCA for his Sunday basketball game, and she stayed with the baby. Though it threw off the numbers not to have her, he was grateful for the time.

He had a new respect for his mother. On his drive home, he'd vowed that every Mother's Day he would spoil her more. And he thought he'd send her flowers every week too. There just weren't enough holidays to honor her.

Now he sat in his daughter's bedroom rocking her in the chair that Ray and his children had gifted her. It had been Ray's ex-wife Kelly's idea to give them the chair. She'd refinished it when she'd been pregnant with their oldest, and she thought it would be the perfect gift for Alex.

He wasn't sure how many thank you notes he'd written in the past two weeks, including one to Kelly and the kids, but he hoped to thank her someday in person.

When the bedroom door opened softly, Sarah peeked her head in. "There's someone here to see you."

"Someone?"

"Yeah," she said as she opened the door fully and Catherine

stepped past her and into the room.

Sarah smiled and shut the door.

The air suddenly filled with worry, and he wondered if Celia Rose felt it too because she stirred.

"Hi," he whispered as he adjusted his daughter in his arms.

"Hi."

"I wasn't expecting to see you," he said softly, realizing that he hadn't shaved in over a week, his hair was much too long, and he hadn't changed since he'd been home from playing basketball.

"I didn't know I was coming. It's as if my car drove me here, and when I came to, I was parked outside your house. That sounds made up, but I feel as if there is some truth to it."

Alex couldn't help but smile up at her. "I'm glad you're here. I've wanted you to meet her."

"She's beautiful. I got your card and your picture. I hung it on my fridge."

And that was positive, he thought. His gaze moved to her hand, and he noticed that the ring wasn't on her finger. Well, he couldn't have everything, he decided.

She must have noticed his gaze, and she wrapped her arms around herself. "You look natural."

"Who ever would have thought that I'd figure it out this fast, huh? Would you like to hold her?"

Catherine's eyes went wide and she shook her head. "Oh, I don't think so. I should go. You have a lot to do."

Alex stood with Celia Rose in his arms. "Sit. I need to change clothes. I just wanted to snuggle with her as soon as I got home," he admitted.

"Maybe Sarah…"

"Catherine, sit down."

Setting her purse on the floor, Catherine walked across the room and took the chair he'd been occupying. Slowly, Alex laid Celia Rose in her arms.

He'd heard the inhale as he'd done so and saw the glimmer of tears welling in her eyes. "I'll be right back. Can I get you something to drink?"

Without looking up at him, she shook her head.

He pulled the door closed slightly and walked to the kitchen.

Sarah looked up at him from her computer. "What are you doing?"

"I'm letting them bond."

"Is she here to stay?"

Alex shrugged. "But they need a moment to get to know each other," he said before turning toward his bedroom.

"You are beautiful," he heard Catherine's voice and realized that the baby monitor on his night stand was on. "You have your daddy's lips, and his eyes. Well, I saw those in the photo. Maybe you'll show me them before I leave."

Alex sat down on his bed and listened. He shouldn't have, but he couldn't help it.

"I haven't been nice to your daddy. But I do love him. Maybe someday he'll forgive me. I know he made the right decision." She sighed. "There was no decision. He knew what he had to do."

Alex kicked off his shoes and pulled a pair of lounging pants from the drawer as he heard the familiar sound of Celia Rose stirring. It appeared that Catherine was about to see those big brown eyes.

"Oh, that's a big stretch," she said and Alex's heart melted just a bit knowing how adorable that moment was. "There's those big brown eyes. Yep, just like your daddy's."

He pulled off his shirt and took a clean one from the drawer. As he pulled it on, he heard Celia Rose coo. She was happy in Catherine's arms.

God, how could he possibly convince her, now that she'd taken off the ring, that Celia Rose needed her as much as he did.

Before he went back into the bedroom, he stopped in the kitchen, pulled two bottles of water from the refrigerator, and kissed his sister on the top of her head.

. . .

WHEN THE DOOR OPENED, CATHERINE LOOKED UP AT ALEX, NOW changed from his basketball attire into lounging clothes. Then she looked down at the baby she held in her arms, whose hands moved and her tongue darted in and out of her rosebud lips.

"Well, there's your daddy. I think it's time for me to go," she whispered.

"I wish you'd stay."

"I probably shouldn't have even come."

Alex set the water bottles on the dresser and moved to kneel in front of Catherine and Celia Rose. "You should have never left," he said and then winced when he did. "I'm sorry." He ran his hand over his daughter's head. "I just miss you."

"You're too busy to be missing me now."

"No. That void wasn't filled with this. That void only grew deeper."

Catherine lifted the baby to her shoulder and rubbed her back, as she looked into Alex's sad eyes. "She needs you."

"And I need you." Reaching for Celia Rose, he took her from Catherine's shoulder, and placed her on his. Then, as he stood, he took Catherine's hand and pulled her from the chair. "We need you. Every decision I ever make will have her in it from here on. She doesn't stop me from having my own happiness, and she doesn't stop me from wanting to love someone. She lost too. I'm all she has, and we all know what a shitty lot in life that is."

Catherine couldn't help but chuckle at that.

When his finger came under her chin, she looked up into his eyes—those eyes that held love deep in them.

"Come back around more often. I would like her to grow up with you around."

Celia Rose lifted her head, and Catherine rested her hand on her back. She had some seriously big decisions to make.

*a*lex sat on the sofa after having put Celia Rose to bed. Sarah had gone to her house to gather her mail from the past few days, water her plants, and clean out her refrigerator.

When she walked in the back door, Alex stood and walked to the kitchen.

He moved to her quickly, noticing her juggling grocery bags that hung from every finger.

"What is all of this?" he asked taking some of the bags.

"I had just gone to the store before we left for Baltimore. If we don't eat this it'll all go to waste."

He opened the refrigerator and began to unload one of the bags. "How do you think it went with Catherine today?" he asked and he heard his sister huff.

"Why are you asking me? You know, I'm pissed at her. You don't deserve this little game she's playing."

He shook his head. "I don't think it's a game. Celia Rose is mine. To Catherine, she's part Cara's too."

"Well, she is."

"I know." He let out a breath. "But I get it."

"Rachel was right. You're an asshole for being so nice. I think you should go over and give her a piece of your mind. She needs to decide if she's in or out. You know Celia Rose only slightly better than she does. I'm not saying Celia Rose needs a mother, but Catherine would be an excellent one. And she puts up with your shit." She let out a groan. "Well she did, before you became the sensible one."

Alex laughed at his sister's comments. Did she realize she was talking in circles?

"You think I should still fight for her?"

Sarah pulled items from the bag on the table and passed by him to put them in the open refrigerator. "I think she mixed the message when she showed up here."

He'd admit that was true.

Sarah closed the refrigerator door and leaned up against it. "But if it were me, I would think that her coming by was her feeling it out. She needed to see Celia Rose for herself. She needed to touch her, smell her, and know that she's not a threat. But I also think she's made enough of an ass of herself that she's embarrassed. How do you come back from that?"

"She didn't have her ring on."

"I noticed." Sarah moved back to the table and emptied another bag. "I don't know. I just think it would be a shame if I'm the only one who gets to know that little girl better than anyone —except you."

"You think I should go talk to her?"

"I think you should stop letting me ramble on and go."

When the back door opened again, Bruce walked through and stepped into the kitchen. "I have to admit, it's nice to have people back in the house."

"I hope Celia Rose doesn't keep you up at night," Alex said.

"Not at all. She gives the atmosphere a boost."

Sarah turned toward Bruce, hands on her hips, and cast a look toward Alex. "Catherine came by today and met Celia Rose."

Bruce's eyes widened. "She's back? I mean, that's good, right?"

Alex shrugged. "She just dropped by."

Sarah threw her hands in the air. "Will you tell him he's being stupid and he should go to her and talk to her?"

Bruce opened his mouth to speak, and then exchanged glances with Sarah again, who nodded.

"If she came here, I think it's a step. Just because you gained a daughter, I don't think you should lose a fiancée," Bruce said. "I think you should go talk to her."

When he said that, Sarah moved to Bruce and kissed him hard on the mouth. "Thank you."

Of course that little move didn't settle well with Alex at all, but he had to assume that was his sister's motive behind it.

"Fine. I'll go."

Bruce looked at his watch. "It's ten o'clock."

"Well, do I go or not?"

Sarah pulled his keys from the key rack and placed them in Alex's hand. "If I have to be more blunt that this, you're dumber than I thought. Celia Rose is in good hands. I'll take care of her. We have plenty of breast milk and formula too, in case it takes you all night long," she said with a wink.

Alex kissed his sister on the cheek and passed by Bruce before turning back to him. "Off limits," he whispered.

"Can't help it if she wants me," Bruce replied with a wink.

At that moment, it wasn't even worth having the conversation with him. He was on a mission to get his fiancée back.

CHAPTER 46

*J*t was silly, but Catherine hadn't even changed out of her shirt when she'd climbed into bed. She could still smell Celia Rose's scent, and for some reason it gave her some comfort.

It was hard to watch Alex look at his daughter with eyes that were filled with so much love. And that was selfish, because when he'd looked into Catherine's eyes, there was love there too.

She thought about what Alex had said about Celia Rose having already lost. She would never—ever know her mother. It wasn't as if she'd left her on purpose, but she wouldn't be coming back.

There was an opportunity for Catherine to make a difference in a life, and was she up for that challenge? Alex had told her he loved her and missed her. There was room for forgiveness there, she thought.

Holding her shirt to her nose, and thinking of how silly it was to be obsessing about the baby, she sniffed back tears.

Celia Rose was Alex's flesh and blood. If they did get married, their babies would be Celia Rose's flesh and blood too.

She jumped when her phone buzzed on the night stand. There was a text from Alex, and it was eleven o'clock.

Her heart raced as she sat up and slid her finger over the screen of her phone to open the message.

What are you doing?

Seriously? This was what he did in his spare time now?

Nothing, she replied.

When she heard the knock at the front door, she nearly let out a scream. He was there?

Kicking her feet over the edge of the bed, she freed herself from the sheets that had tangled around her and ran down the steps. The security alarm screeched as she pulled open the door.

"Shit!" she turned to the pad and punched in the numbers as he laughed.

When she turned back to the door, there he stood with a bouquet of flowers in his hand, looking absolutely adorable with his hair falling over his forehead, and a nearly full beard. Parenthood seemed to make him sexier.

"What are you doing here? Where's your daughter? You didn't leave her in the car did you?"

He smiled and held the flowers out to her. "She's with her auntie and in good hands. These are for you. Thank goodness grocery stores are open late."

"You drove all the way over here to give these to me?"

Now he stepped through the door and Catherine took a step back to let him in. "No, I came here to give you this," he said as he cupped her face in his hands and lowered his mouth to hers.

This was confusing, and she considered pulling away, but she couldn't. It had been a long two weeks, and all she could think about was his kisses, his touches, and just being near him.

"Alex..."

"Don't do that. Don't ignore what's really going on."

"And what's going on?"

He kissed her again, and this time she had to wrap her arms around his neck to stay upright.

"I love you."

Catherine pressed her forehead to his. "I love you too."

"Then marry me. My daughter would like you to be her mommy." He kissed her again. "She'd like you to be there when she wakes up." He kissed her neck. "She'd like you to be there during play time." He moved a kiss over her collarbone. "She'd like brothers and sisters to play with."

Now the air stuck in her lungs and she had to ease back. "My head is spinning," she said and he smiled down at her.

"Good. You don't think right when your head isn't spinning." He kissed her again before he hoisted her to his hips, and she wrapped her legs around him. "Marry me," he said again before covering her mouth with his and carrying her up the stairs.

When he laid her back on her bed and moved in on top of her, she knew she'd lost the battle, but the battle was within her, and it wasn't with Alex at all.

"We need to talk," she said between his kisses as she pressed her hands to his chest.

"We're talking."

His hands rose under her shirt and she sucked in a breath. Maybe they should just talk after—but no. She had to focus.

"Things changed," she said as he cupped her breast in his hand.

"They sure did." His tongue skimmed her bottom lip. "They changed a lot. I have a baby."

"Right."

"She's amazing, but really, talking about her isn't helping."

That made Catherine laugh. "It's a forever commitment."

"It is. So was agreeing to marriage," he reminded her before he lifted her shirt and covered her breast with his mouth.

"Alex," she sighed as she lifted his face so that his eyes were on hers. "Do you really want to marry me?"

He let out a laugh. "What do you think I'm doing here?"

"Distracting me."

"Okay, that too." Now he gently placed a kiss on her lips. "I really do want to marry you. Just as much as I did before I'd heard the name Celia Rose."

"What if she hates me?"

"At some point your own children will hate you," he acknowledged. "She will love you. I heard you talking to her today. I kind of think you love her too."

Catherine pushed him back so that she could see him clearer. "You heard me?"

He shrugged. "The baby monitor was on."

She closed her eyes and laughed. "I left my shirt on because I could smell her on it."

"I think you fell in love with her as quickly as I did."

"I've been horrible about this."

"You have been, and it's understandable."

"It was selfish."

"It was sudden."

"Rachel has let me know how petty I've been, but I already knew that."

Alex eased on his elbow and brushed a strand of hair from her face. "With everything that has changed in the past two weeks, the one thing that never changed for me was loving you. Let me ask again, Catherine, would you please marry me?"

She could feel the hot tears roll from her eyes. Telling him yes would mean that she would instantly be a mother too—but hadn't she wanted that with him all along?

And Celia Rose—he was right, the moment he'd put her in Catherine's arms, she'd fallen in love.

It was now or never. If she turned him away, he might walk for good. If she told him yes, she recommitted herself to the only man she'd ever loved, and she would become the mother to his baby girl.

"You're thinking too hard again," he said.

"I don't want to wait until Rachel can fit into a dress."

The corner of Alex's mouth curled up. "Tell me. What do you want?"

Catherine rolled Alex onto his back and straddled him. His hands came to her hips as he smiled up at her.

"I want your last name. I want your daughter to call me Mom. I want two more babies, and I want to start tonight."

"Say it, Catherine. What do you want?"

"Marry me tomorrow, Alex. I don't want to wait."

"Where is your ring?"

Catherine slid off the bed and walked toward the dresser. She lifted the lid from a small container and pulled out the ring. Alex sat up and took the ring when she handed it to him.

"Catherine Anderson, I would be honored to marry you tomorrow if you'll love me and have me forever."

The tears rolled over her cheeks. "I will love you and have you forever, I promise."

"And you'll take my daughter as your own?"

"I will."

"And you were serious about wanting more babies—tonight?"

"Now we're just wasting time," she teased as Alex pushed the ring on her finger. "When will Celia Rose wake up?"

He chuckled. "She'll wake up two or three times. But she'll be up by six."

"Then we'd better stop talking and get busy. I want to be there when my daughter wakes up tomorrow. I want to buy her a new dress before our wedding."

"You'll marry me?" he asked one more time.

"I'll marry you."

EPILOGUE

*A*t the first sound of movement on the baby monitor, Catherine sat up in Alex's bed, and he followed.

"There you go," he said, softly resting his hand on her shoulder. "She's ready for you."

Catherine batted her heavy and tired eyes, having only crawled into Alex's bed two hours earlier.

She set her feet on the floor and walked through the dark house. Turning on the small lamp on the dresser, she watched Celia Rose wiggle in her wrap.

"Good morning, sweetheart," she said softly as she moved toward her crib.

Those big brown eyes batted open and looked up at her, and a moment later, she smiled at Catherine, and in that moment she knew Alex was right. She'd fallen in love with Celia Rose.

She unwrapped the sleepy baby and lifted her from the crib. Again, the smell of her filled her as she held Celia Rose to her chest.

"I love you, little one. I love your daddy too. I promise to be here for you, forever."

ALEX TOOK IT UPON HIMSELF TO CALL RAY AND ASK FOR ONE MORE day for Catherine. He heard the irritation in Ray's voice, but he'd agreed.

"Be at my house at five," he told Ray before he disconnected the call. "I need to talk to you all."

The same cryptic call was made to all of their friends and family. At this point, he wondered what they might all be thinking, but he'd needed some humor, Alex thought.

Catherine had gone shopping that morning, and was dressing Celia Rose and herself in whatever she had bought.

When they emerged in matching dresses, Alex's heart squeezed in his chest. How could he possibly hold so much love for both of them, but he did. And seeing them together only intensified it.

"You both look beautiful," he said as he moved to them and pressed a kiss to both of their cheeks.

"We're ready, Daddy," Catherine said as she kissed Celia Rose on the top of the head.

"Our appointment is in an hour. It'll take us that long to get downtown and get her in and out of the car," he teased.

"Let's go."

IT WAS NO SURPRISE WHEN RACHEL WAS THE FIRST ONE TO THE door. Alex opened it, and she rushed past him. "What's going on? What's wrong with Celia Rose? Everyone is pulling up at the same time. You were awfully cryptic about why we're here," she continued as she rested her hands on her stomach.

Alex pulled her to him and kissed her on the cheek. "I'll tell you in a minute."

"I don't like these games, Burke."

"Just be patient."

Just as Rachel had said, everyone was pulling up at the same time and filing into the living room. All of the same questions were asked and with a smile on his face, Alex offered everyone a seat.

It wasn't until Bruce came up the back steps and shouted, "What's the cake in the kitchen for?" before he saw the room full of people that everyone assumed they were there for bad news.

Alex laughed. "Sit down, would you? I'll be right back."

With all of their friends and their family gathered in the living room, Alex walked to his bedroom and opened the door.

"Are you ready?" he asked as Catherine bounced a wide eyed Celia Rose on her hip.

"We're ready," she said.

Alex took their daughter, still in the dress her mother had dressed her in that morning, and held her to his chest. With his other hand, he interlaced fingers with his wife and they walked to the other room.

When he entered the room with Catherine, there was a collective sound. He assumed there was surprise, and maybe some shock, which probably came from her mother.

Sarah was the first to speak. "What are you two up to?"

Alex wrapped his arm around Catherine's waist and pulled her in close.

"The past two weeks have been a little strenuous," he said as he exchanged looks with Catherine. "But the reason we gathered you here today, and the reason there is a cake in the kitchen," he directed the statement toward Bruce, "is because last night, Catherine agreed to be Celia Rose's mother."

That statement alone brought Rachel and Sarah to their feet. But before they could rush them, Alex held up a hand, and then gathered Catherine in close again.

"And because we didn't want to wait a minute longer to be a family, Catherine and I, and Celia Rose, got married today."

Now Rachel raced to them, and Sarah was on her heels.

"Oh my God!" Rachel kissed Catherine's cheek. "You did? You got married without me?" They both laughed. "But you did?" she repeated the question.

"We did. I love them both. How could I not want that to start right away?"

Rachel gathered Catherine up in her arms. "I'm so glad you got your head out of your ass."

Rachel then moved to Alex. "You wore her down," she teased as she lifted on her toes to kiss his cheek. "I'm so happy for you both—all three of you," she corrected.

W̲HEN THEY'D CELEBRATED WITH THEIR FAMILY, AND ENJOYED THE cake, Catherine and Alex sat on the couch with their daughter.

"I'll never be able to apologize for my attitude the past two weeks," she said as she touched Celia Rose's cheek as she slept in her father's arms. "It wasn't as if you'd done this to me on purpose, and it would have probably been much easier had I been more supportive."

"The point is we're together now. A family." He pressed a kiss to her lips. "And don't forget, you were the one last night begging to start growing our family."

Catherine laughed as she rested her head to his shoulder. "I'm ready to fill this house," she said. "Perhaps we'd better ask Bruce to move into my place."

"The further away he is from my sister, the better."

Catherine tucked her finger into Celia Rose's tiny hand. "I do love her," she said. "I promise to honor her mother."

Alex kissed the top of Catherine's head. "She'll always know who her mother was, and she'll always know you loved her from the beginning." Celia Rose stretched, and they both watched. "One thing I've learned, no matter how easy and wonderful it is to sit and watch her, we should put her to bed. She'll be awake in a few hours, and a few after that. Besides, your boss needs you back to work."

Catherine lifted their daughter from her father's arms and stood. "I'll put her down. But don't go to sleep. I'm on my honey-moon, and I want an hour with my husband."

We hope you enjoyed book one in the Funerals and Weddings Series, *Something Discovered.*
Please enjoy an excerpt from book three,
Something Found.

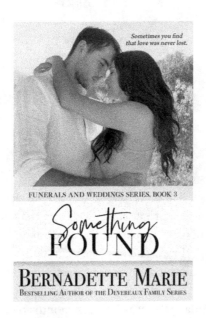

Sometimes you find
that love was never lost.

FUNERALS AND WEDDINGS SERIES, BOOK 3

Something
FOUND

BERNADETTE MARIE
BESTSELLING AUTHOR OF THE DEVEREAUX FAMILY SERIES

SOMETHING FOUND

*P*iles of plans and blueprints covered the top of Ray's desk. It was the season to plan out new builds which would begin in the spring. He'd picked up the contract on new multi-story condos, a city park, and a medical building.

He lifted his head when he saw Catherine walk from her office to the break room, no doubt for another cup of coffee. Life with an infant wasn't easy, he remembered.

Catherine's daughter was now six months old, but Catherine had only recently become her mother. Had she given birth to her, she'd have been prepared for sleepless nights. As it was, Celia Rose was an unexpected gift.

Ray swiveled his chair toward his computer to begin an email when Catherine walked into his office with two mugs of coffee.

"I thought you might want one," she said as she handed him one of the mugs and set down an orange wrapped piece of candy.

"Thank you." He took the coffee from her and the piece of candy, which Catherine had brought in to the office in an attempt to rid herself of extra Halloween candy at home. "Long night?"

"Celia Rose is trying to get her first tooth," she said as she yawned. "Alex had an early meeting, so I took night duty last night."

He remembered when he and his ex-wife would share the baby duties at night. That seemed so long ago now.

"I know this sounds like the standard response, but enjoy it. It goes so fast."

Catherine sipped her coffee. "I'm trying to absorb everything. Not getting to be part of her first five months, I want to remember all of it. It'll be different when we have more kids and I'm part of their creation process. But I want to be able to tell her everything."

"I assume you'll be at the YMCA on Sunday for basketball?"

"Yeah. Alex really missed those few weeks. He's been glad to get back to it. And I think that Celia Rose is ready for that kind of commotion," she smiled wide as she spoke of her daughter.

"I have the kids this week, and I know Charlotte is dying to see her again."

"Then I'll make sure we're there," she agreed as Allen at the front desk called to her to inform her that she had a phone call. "I guess my coffee break is over."

Ray watched as she walked back to her office. He was happy for Catherine and Alex. A new marriage and a new baby, it brought back a lot of memories.

He and Kelly had been divorced for two years, but they were amicable. He might even venture to say they were better friends than they had been before they got married.

They shared the kids and the responsibilities, only he lived in a different house, and not the one he'd bought.

Not everything turned out the way things were planned.

He sipped the coffee Catherine had handed him, and looked at the clock. It was ten-thirty. If he planned on getting through that stack on his desk in the next four hours, he needed to make a move. Kelly would bring the kids to the office after school.

It was a good thing they were amicable, because on his weeks with the kids, he saw his ex-wife every day when she'd drop them off after school.

Allen poked his head through the office door. "Kelly is on line one," he said.

Ray chuckled and looked at his watch. Day one of his week with the kids always started with the call during Kelly's planning period at school to make sure he knew what he was doing.

He'd been parenting their kids as long as she had, but Kelly always had an organization to her that led her to making him feel inferior. He wasn't going to forget things. He wasn't going to miss a step. But, he was about to take his bi-weekly phone call that assured that.

"Hey, Kel, what's up?" he said as he answered the phone.

On the other end of the line, he heard the familiar sigh since he'd shortened her name. "Got ten minutes?"

"Ten? This usually takes five."

"Ray, just hear me out."

He leaned back in his chair and closed his eyes. "Go on."

"Charlotte had a cough this morning. It went away before school, but if it gets worse she'll have to stay home. Do you have Dr. Goodman's phone number?"

"Same doctor she's had since she was born?"

"Yes."

"Then, yeah, I have it."

"Don't let her around the baby if she's coughing." Wasn't that a given? "And call me if—"

"I got it," he bit out. "Continue."

He heard the inhale of frustration. "Connor is supposed to bring a treat to share on Friday that he made following a recipe. Now, I can keep him on Thursday and—"

"I can follow a recipe, Kel. What's next?"

"My mother's birthday—"

"Is on Wednesday. The kids will video call her on Wednesday night at six, does that work?"

"Ray…"

"I told you. I got this," he said as he sat up and put his feet on the ground. "You act like I don't know how to handle my own kids. We have this down, and have for two years. You let me see them on your weeks, and you see them at school, so you can check up on them. You and I can share a meal without a fight, and the kids are well adjusted. These phone calls of yours could be summed up in an email with dates, or you can tell me when you drop them off, and I'll handle it."

She was silent for a moment. "Fine. I don't mean to bother you when I call you."

Ray let out a breath. It was never a bother, and he shouldn't have responded like that. "I'm sorry. I'm going over contracts and budgets. Maybe I'm a little testy. What else?"

"Full day kindergarten has Connor exhausted." Which he already knew, but no more arguments, he promised himself. "Just make sure he's getting a good dinner and to bed on time. He has his Switch in his backpack, so take it away before bed. I don't know if he'll tell you he has it."

"Understood."

"I think that's it," she said, but Ray wasn't sure it was.

"Are you sure? And I'm not asking to be crappy, I'm asking because you sound preoccupied with another thought."

There was an uncomfortable pause. "Jeremy Cross asked me to dinner," she said, and the name socked Ray right in the gut.

"Oh, yeah? He'd asked about you the last time I saw him." Of course he did. He'd asked if his hot wife of his was still around, and it looked like he jumped on the news that they were divorced.

"His kids go to my school. I took his invite."

Ray winced. "I hope he takes you somewhere nice. What else do I need to know?"

"That's it. I'll have the kids to you by three."

"I can't wait."

PLEASE REVIEW

We hope you enjoyed Something Discovered by Bernadette Marie. If you did, we would ask that you please rate and review this title. Every review helps our authors.

Rate and Review: Something Discovered

5 Prince Publishing
Arvada, Colorado, USA

MEET THE AUTHOR

Bestselling Author Bernadette Marie is known for building families readers want to be part of. Her series The Keller Family has graced bestseller charts since its release in 2011. Since then she has authored and published over forty-five books. The married mother of five sons promises romances with a Happily Ever After always...and says she can write it because she lives it.

Obsessed with the art of writing and the business of publishing, chronic entrepreneur Bernadette Marie established her own publishing house, 5 Prince Publishing, in 2011 to bring her own work to market as well as offer an opportunity for fresh voices in fiction to find a home as well.

When not immersed in the writing/publishing world, Bernadette Marie can be found spending time with her family, traveling, and running multiple businesses. An avid martial artist, Bernadette Marie is a second degree black belt in Tang Soo Do, and loves Tai Chi. She is a retired hockey mom, a lover of a good stout craft beer, and might have an unhealthy addiction to chocolate.

CPSIA information can be obtained
at www.ICGtesting.com
Printed in the USA
BVHW031014041021
618090BV00005B/134